"I'm Pierce Masterson,"
the stranger said, wiping his palm on
his leg before offering her his hand.

Haley looked at his hand and then him. Reluctantly, she took his hand and shook it.

"Haley Sanders," she said. She looked Masterson over from head to toe. What kind of handyman did yard work in dress slacks and designer loafers?

"I'd like to clean up a bit," he said. "I'll be right back."

Haley watched him walk to his car. The sporty sedan seemed a little pricey for a handyman, but her mind went blank when he pulled off his shirt. The door on his car prevented a full-frontal view, but it didn't stop her from seeing his muscular shoulder and powerful chest. Mowing lawns certainly agreed with him.

It wasn't just his body that made her long for a cold drink of water on this cloudless, warm day. His handsome profile completed the package. Suddenly, all she could think about was that her new handyman was one mouthwatering piece of eye candy....

MICHELLE MONKOU

became a world traveler at the age of three when she left her birthplace of London, England, and moved to Guyana, South America. She then moved to the United States as a young teen. An avid reader, her love of books mixed with her cultural experiences and set the tone for her vivid imagination. It wasn't long before the stories in her head became novels on paper. Michelle enjoys writing heartfelt, satisfying romances. Visit her Web site, www.michellemonkou.com, or write to P.O. Box 2904, Laurel, MD 20709 or e-mail at michellemonkou@comcast.net.

MICHELLE MONKOU

Sweet Surrender

To my big sis, Angela Gordon, we're on this crazy ride together—Onward and Upward!

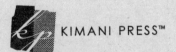 KIMANI PRESS™

ISBN-13: 978-1-58314-780-1
ISBN-10:   1-58314-780-2

SWEET SURRENDER

www.kimanipress.com

Printed in U.S.A.

Dear Reader,

I'm excited to participate in Harlequin's new Kimani Press imprint. After growing up on Harlequin romances in the seventies and eighties, I couldn't be more thrilled to write one.

With equal enthusiasm, I bring you the Masterson family. Each sibling has distinctive characteristics that might be called quirky, independent, strong or opinionated. Yet, underlying the family's foundation is their bond and support for each other after suffering a shared, troubled childhood. I look forward to bringing you each story of erupting conflicts, satisfying resolutions and titillating romances.

Join me on the journey. Share your thoughts on this family and more. Visit my Web site and register for contests and other information, www.michellemonkou.com, write to P.O. Box 2904, Laurel, MD 20709 or e-mail at michellemonkou@comcast.net.

Here's wishing that your dreams come true.

Michelle Monkou

Chapter 1

Haley Sanders sealed the last moving box and pushed it against the wall. The word *kitchen* had been scrawled on its sides to make the eventual unpacking easier.

She'd spent the last three days throwing away or packing possessions in her two-bedroom apartment that had been home for exactly one year. Muscles in her shoulders and lower back protested each movement. Tonight her body would demand payback when her muscles tightened and ached to the bone.

There could be no stopping now.

She glanced over the open kitchen and tiny living area, a far cry from the mini-mansion in buppie-dom, Mitchellville, Maryland. No custom-designed mini-blinds decorated the windows. The standard white paint had no colorful border accents to pick up the coordinated scheme in the carpet and furniture.

But there had been no way that she could have remained living in the house that had seen the early giddy days of her married life, the birth of her only child and had witnessed her husband's acts of intimate betrayal. After the legal separation, she'd endured six months under that hellish roof until she could afford to move.

Her little apartment had become more than home. It was the place where everyone reassured her that she'd move on with her life. The healing was far from complete, though. It wouldn't be until she could put distance between herself and her past.

Trying to keep herself busy, she picked up a cloth and the multipurpose spray cleaner. The landlord would be up soon for the final walk-through. She sprayed at the random smudges on the wall, erasing traces of her existence in the kitchen, bathroom and bedroom.

In the master bedroom, her new queen-size bed sat bare. The bed had been the first item she'd intended to replace. Thinking about lying on the mattress that she'd shared with her husband and his other woman still had the power to make her stomach heave.

She fiddled with the thin gold band on her wedding finger. The intricate, diamond-studded wedding ring set had long been replaced with a simple gold band. Those who knew she was divorced accepted her explanation that the ring kept men from approaching her.

However, the metal served as a talisman to ward off another relationship. As she slid the band around her finger, she stared at her hand. Once in a while she indulged in a manicure, but most times, like today, her fingernails were short and unpolished.

Sliding the ring to her knuckle, she looked at the untanned skin. The pale line against her toffee-colored complexion had the same effect as a flashing neon sign overhead announcing her failure.

She couldn't make it as a wife and had failed as a lover.

"Hey, Mom. You okay?"

"Of course." Haley quickly dropped her hand to her side. She blinked back the sting of tears.

Her daughter stood in the doorway. Her lean body on the brink of maturity sported a crop top and jeans low on her hips.

"Did you do a quick run-through of your room?" Haley pasted a bright smile to erase her daughter's visible unease at seeing her upset. Throughout this ordeal, she'd made it a point not to show any signs that she couldn't handle the divorce.

"Are you sure we're going to get help to load these boxes?"

"Yes, Beth." Haley smiled. "Your uncles are coming." She glanced at her watch. "Anytime now." She crossed the room and placed an arm around her daughter's shoulders.

"Yeah, right." Beth shrugged off the offending arm and headed to the front door. "I'll be outside."

"Don't go far. As soon as everything is on the truck, we're leaving."

Beth surveyed the room. "If you think so."

Haley watched the front door close. "Smart-ass." Since she'd told Beth they were moving, Beth had kept her at arm's distance. Obviously, nothing had changed. But she was determined that things would get better soon. The forbidden clothes would have to be dealt with later.

Where were her brothers? She should've known better. But there was no one else to ask. She walked to the wall phone in the kitchen. Never mind that she'd already placed two calls. Her brothers didn't budge unless she nagged them incessantly. Today proved to be no exception.

Her eldest brother, Theo, had a nasty reputation for being unfashionably late. No one bothered him about it. His pit-bull physique and tree-trunk limbs tempered any person's irritation.

On the other hand, the middle sibling, Stan, was punctual, except when one of his many girlfriends distracted him. He called himself the Love Doctor and declared himself on call twenty-four hours, seven days a week for his lady friends.

As the little sister, she didn't carry too much clout. Haley prepared to make yet another call when the doorbell sounded.

"Thank goodness," she muttered. Maybe she wouldn't be too off her schedule. A two-hour drive remained in front of her.

She opened the door. "What took you so—?"

"Hello, Haley."

"Vernon?" Haley's grip tightened on the

doorknob. She'd already stepped back in welcome, expecting her brothers to enter. Her ex-husband acted on the unintended invitation and strode with heavy steps into the living room.

"Where's Beth?" he asked over his shoulder. His focus zeroed in on the stacked boxes.

"Why are you here?" Damn the shakiness in her voice. She didn't move from the door, nor did she close it. Only his profile was in view. His tight, controlled movements reminded her of a tiger swishing his tail, sizing up the lay of the surroundings before launching in attack.

"Did you think you could sneak out of town with my daughter?"

Haley heard the steely edge lacing his words. She knew from experience that his fury wasn't too far behind. Though he'd never lifted a hand against her, he'd blasted away her confidence with his tongue enough times to set her on automatic alert with the occasional retreat.

"You look a mess." He faced her with arms folded across his chest. His disgust poured onto her and clung like a thick, oily coating. "Why would *you* wear shorts? First, you're too old to dress like a teenager. Second, you need to set an example for my daughter. Third, it sure looks like you haven't kept up with the jogging program I designed for you. Take my advice, visit a gym."

Her teeth worked on the inner side of her lip. Red-hot anger swallowed her entire face, shooting its way to the roots of her hair. Anger and a double serving of embarrassment warred with her emotions, a constant state of her reality whenever Vernon was around.

She'd love to have the courage to call him names, but he was always the picture of perfection with a toned physique outfitted in designer clothing. He always managed to look as if he had stepped out of the shower, fresh and clean, wearing perfectly creased pants and crisp shirts. Vernon had always been neat and a control freak.

She leaned against the open door for support and as a possible route of escape. Her ability to think rationally had gone into sleep mode, with the defensive flight mode activated.

"Vernon, we have nothing to discuss. I don't have to tell you when and where I'm going. I have full custody of Beth and as agreed, you will see her a week in the summer and Thanksgiving." To her ears she sounded breathless, as if she had sprinted around a track.

"No court is going to decide when I can see

my own daughter." He took a step toward her. "Where is she?"

"She's not here." She tried to match his arrogance, but couldn't keep her eyes locked with his. Too much anger shone back at her. A long time ago, it used to be love, or something close to it.

"Going out of state?"

"Maybe," she hedged.

He raised her chin with his finger. "Look at me."

She didn't.

"I said, look at me."

She slowly moved her eyes up his face until she stared back at familiar cold eyes that were dark enough to be considered black. "You don't have to tell me where you're going because I can afford to find you anywhere, anytime. I took care of you. I made you a woman. Gave you my family's name. You were nothing before you met me. No matter what melodrama is playing in your silly mind, I took good care of you and my daughter like a husband and father should." He leaned closer. "It's not over."

She pulled her chin out of his grasp. Her heart throbbed painfully against her chest. "Either you leave this apartment now or I will."

He stared down at her. Any outward emotion smothered. Only a sneer played on his lips.

Her brothers' noisy approach broke the standoff. She almost sank to her knees with relief.

"You're still my wife. No judge can end our marriage. Like I said, it's not over. You're nothing without me." He walked out of the apartment and past her brothers who had stopped in the middle of their conversation at his unexpected appearance.

"Hey, sis." Theo motioned with his head. "What's up with that?"

"Nothing." Haley didn't feel like going into it. Although the vision of Theo beating Vernon to a pulp appealed to her, she'd end up paying dearly for such a treat.

Now that Vernon had left, her nerves hummed like a live wire. A sickening feeling in the pit of her stomach would more than likely end in heartburn. She gritted her teeth to stem her body's trembling.

Right now, all she wanted was to get the heck out of town.

Vernon's threat continued to bounce around in her head. Her quest to start over in a new city, with a new job, in a new home could all be destroyed by her ex-husband's whim.

She could accept Vernon thinking of her as a frightened rabbit. His approval didn't matter anymore. But Beth deserved stability and a happy home. Nothing else mattered. She'd vowed that Beth wouldn't suffer for the decisions that she'd made to end her marriage and carve out a life for them.

Pierce Masterson sat in the antique office chair that had once been his father's. It wasn't the most comfortable piece in the home office, but he'd seen his reflection in the mirror and it added authority to his appearance.

His relatives were always ready to tell him that he was the younger version of his father without the premature gray hair at his temples that was the signature trademark of the Masterson males. Maybe they thought reminding him of his resemblance to his father stroked his ego. He, on the other hand, hoped the resemblance ended there— on the physical level.

Since his teen years, he had assumed a fatherly role for his younger siblings. His mother had often been working or had been too busy to take care of them after his father had left. He rubbed his temples, priming himself for the fight ahead.

He could predict to the minutest detail how this family meeting would go.

Now his younger siblings sat in the room staring at him. Their anticipation pressed him to speak. He needed his two sisters to understand his decision. There was no other solution. Meanwhile, his younger brother and the baby of the family could barely keep his life together, much less be tapped for his opinion on the matter.

"I don't know what else you expect me to say. We're getting nowhere with this bickering. What I'm proposing makes sense." He refrained from adding *as usual.*

"Makes sense to who?"

"It's *whom,* boy." Pierce glared at the youngest Masterson. Omar had clearly been an oops by his parents when they'd had him twelve years after Pierce. "You've piddled at nothing since coming out with that so-called degree."

"Not everyone wants to be a muckety-muck doctor." Omar stuck his fingers in his pants waist as if he wore suspenders and puffed up his chest. "I'm interested in teaching high-school physical education."

"It took four years and hard cash for you to learn how to tell kids to do jumping jacks?"

"Ease up, Pierce." Sheena, the older of his two sisters, raised her hand. "Omar, I do think it's important that you think about going back to school. It's important for your future. Getting a four-year degree doesn't give you as much leverage as it used to."

"And how would you know, Sheena? You didn't even make it through your four years before you got married to Carlton and had Carlton junior eight months later. Oh yeah, don't tell me—prematurely." He threw an exaggerated wink at her.

Pierce bit his cheek to keep from smiling. He didn't want to encourage Omar. His younger brother always fought dirty when pressed. "Don't try to shift the attention from you," Pierce admonished. "No one is telling you to become a doctor. But we can't carry you while you dabble with a part-time job."

"Omar, didn't you say that you wanted to be a lawyer?" asked Laura, his younger sister. Laura couldn't stand their family *discussions*.

"For heaven's sake, Laura, a lawyer?" Pierce had never seen Omar pick up a book, much less imagined him making it through a reputable law school. Anything less would be a waste of time.

"I wasn't really planning on the legal route. But since Mr. High-and-Mighty over here wants to look down his nose at me, I'll show him that I can be a lawyer."

"This is so like you to do things for the wrong reason." Pierce didn't have the patience to indulge his brother's adolescent fantasy to outdo him. "I've got mounds of paperwork to go through. So let's get this family meeting wrapped up. Omar, you need to think about a serious profession. Get back to me in the next couple of days with a concrete plan for your future." He took a deep breath and turned to his sisters. "Now, let's discuss other important matters. Sheena and Laura, I've made the decision to sell the house. I'll need you to look at—"

"Hold up!" Sheena shot up from her seat. With one hand on her hip, she angrily gestured at him. "You made the decision?" She looked down at Laura. "Do you hear this crap?"

Laura did her wobble-head routine, which meant that she didn't want to commit to nodding or shaking her head. Her nickname was Swiss Miss for her die-hard neutrality.

"I'm the executor, Sheena. I've always made

the decisions for this family. You get emotional and stop thinking. Give it a day and you'll see that I made the best decision." Pierce's gut told him that Sheena would be his biggest objector.

"Not everything in life is clean and logical," Sheena argued.

"I think you're being dramatic for the sake of being dramatic."

Omar chuckled, earning a pointed glare from his sister.

"Just because you've made all the decisions for the family doesn't mean that we can't have our say. We aren't kids anymore. That house is our mother's house. It's where she was born. How can you up and decide that we should get rid of it?"

"One. None of us lives in the house. Two. It's been vacant for over a year since Mom's death. Three. The money can go toward Omar's education."

"Shut up, Pierce. Now I'm mad enough to lay you out flat." Sheena stomped back and forth in front of his desk. Her hands punctuated each word. "That's where we grew up."

"The house is not an ornament you keep around as a memento. I knew you would be emotional about this so I made the decision. I've talked to Laura and she agreed with me to sell."

"You did?" Sheena glared at Laura, who stared at him clearly mortified at his disclosure.

"Sheena, it's for the best. It's for Omar."

Everyone turned their attention to their youngest sibling. Omar didn't resemble his sisters or brother. He was a combination of features shared among them. The latest addition to his constant makeover was a goatee and a thick gold chain around his scrawny neck. He wore his usual uniform: an oversize shirt and wide-legged jeans that looked juvenile, but probably cost more than he had in his pocket, since he was in between jobs.

"Hey, don't pull me into this domestic disaster. As usual, big brother is plowing ahead with his own agenda while we must all bow down to his brilliance and foresight. And of course, we'd be so ungrateful if we didn't remember to say thank you, sir, thank you."

"Enough!" Pierce's fist slammed down on the desk. Omar's blatant disrespect infuriated him.

Omar dropped the expensive lead-crystal paperweight he juggled onto the carpet in response to his brother's outburst.

Sheena stopped. Her mouth parted in mid-stutter.

Laura stared up at him. Her eyes wide like a shocked deer.

"I have never steered you wrong. I've bailed you out of your respective messes on too many occasions." After a deep breath and a moment to compose himself, Pierce continued calmly, "Sheena, my plan is to do a rent-to-own on the property. This way, I can decide if the person is a proper fit before making a final commitment. For your information, I have a woman and a child moving in this weekend." He stood, signaling the end of their meeting. "Any further questions?"

Omar opened his mouth. But Pierce glared at the youngest Masterson until his mouth snapped closed and he retreated out of the room.

"Oh dear, I better go check on him." Laura offered Pierce a shaky smile before running after Omar.

Pierce saw that Sheena hung back. From his periphery, he noticed that she hadn't budged since she'd last spoken. She'd always been the one to test him. She was also the only one who could challenge him when she set her mind to it.

He took a deep breath and prepared himself for

her rage. He wasn't backing down. This subject wasn't up for debate.

He waited for Sheena to begin.

Instead she said nothing, following his pacing with her disdainful gaze until he stopped in front of his desk. "What is it Sheena? I'm not going to argue with you about the house." Impatient, he settled on the edge and folded his arms.

She shook her head. "You've been the big brother. Hell, you were a father when Daddy left. You did a good job."

He nodded. It was the truth, after all.

"But you don't really have a knack for what family is or means."

Her words hit him squarely between the eyes. It stunned him as if she had cursed at him.

"You don't give us credit for making the right decisions. You give yourself credit. All the credit. And you remind us that you handle us and our affairs out of obligation. Not love."

Sheena's complexion could barely be called beige. She was the lightest of them. When she laughed hard or cried, her face took on a pinkish hue. At this moment, he would add the additional descriptive word *hot* to that pinkish hue.

"Love? This isn't one of your chick movies.

This is real life. Seems to me that you've enough emotion for both of us. Your emotions have you struggling with a husband and kid, both a drain on resources, if you ask me."

"And I wouldn't change a thing. What do you have? Your degrees gather dust on the wall. You bought this big house, but it's empty. Not even a casual girlfriend comes to this museum. Your heart is as empty as this house, Pierce." She picked up her pocketbook. "Here's something to chew on. One day you're going to get old. And *we'll* be the ones looking after *you*. You might not care for the sensible and cold-hearted decisions that *we* have to make for *your* good."

Pierce shuddered at the thought of being old and sick in any of their homes.

"I'm leaving now and I really don't want to be around you for a little while." She pushed her hair behind her ears; tears shimmered in her eyes.

"What are you saying?" Sheena had never talked to him in this manner.

"I'm not going to have a shouting match with you. I'm not going to embarrass you with my emotional displays. But I will show you what it feels like not to have someone in your life. So I'm going to take a break from you."

"And by next week, when you need financial help, you'll decide to talk to me." He'd never thrown anything he'd done for her in her face, but her words and her attitude unnerved him. It wasn't cold. It was matter-of-fact. She looked at him like a stranger.

"The next time that I ask you for anything will be when hell freezes over, big brother."

Pierce didn't follow her out to the door, but he heard it snap close. He couldn't move.

An hour later, as the shadows crept across the floor and the room darkened, Pierce still sat on the edge of his desk.

The clock on the mantel broke the silence with its ticking.

He had never felt so alone.

But he had made the right decision. Hadn't he?

Chapter 2

Haley couldn't sleep. She never slept well for the first few nights in strange places. Hotels were the worst, but this new house was no exception. Before she settled in for the night, she had checked and rechecked the locks, windows and placed her sturdy hammer under her pillow. She didn't like guns, so the next best thing was a good, solid weapon.

The house's age, coupled with its expansive wood flooring added to her feelings of creepiness as she lay in the dark. The house creaked and settled, as if searching for a comfortable position. At one point, it sounded as if someone walked down the hall. She tiptoed to the door and eased it open. The hinges on her bedroom door didn't cooperate and emitted a sharp squeak. She wished that her daughter would come running in to sleep with her, but that wasn't going to happen.

This would be a long night, Haley realized as she stared up at the ceiling in the dark. She punched the pillow under her head, frustrated that she couldn't fall asleep. She was supposed to be exhausted.

An animal scurried outside below her bedroom window. Well, it had better be outside. A neighborhood dog barked until a faint voice yelled to shut up. If this kept up, she was heading to the pharmacy for over-the-counter sleeping pills and a night-light. She closed her eyes and started to count sheep.

The bright morning sun peeping through the bedsheets Haley had hung on the windows provided enough of an excuse with its sharp light to get her out of bed. Lots of work lay ahead of her with the brown carton boxes stacked in each room awaiting her attention. Her brothers had positioned the heavy furniture around the house. But once that task had been completed, they'd made their excuses and left, promising to return for her first cookout.

With a loud yawn and lots of stretching, she mentally readied herself to get up and start her new life. She grabbed her robe, jammed her feet into her slippers and headed out of the room.

"Beth?"

Her daughter's room was at the other end of the hallway. A third room was sandwiched between Beth's and Haley's rooms. Beth had grabbed the bigger room and the privacy the moment she'd seen it. She needed her space, as she'd put it.

"Beth!"

No answer.

Haley placed her hand on the doorknob to turn, but hesitated. Opening Beth's door without her consent would be akin to starting World War III. She knocked. Still there was no answer. In a split-second decision, she opened the door. If Beth chose to go berserk, she'd have to remind her that she was the mother in this dynamic duo.

To her surprise, the bed was empty, sheets tossed aside. However, the boxes assigned to the room had been emptied. Beth already had transformed the room into her haven. Haley had to admit that seeing the wooden carving of Beth's name propped on the chest of drawers quieted some of her guilt that simmered below the surface over the move.

She returned to the hallway, looking into the bathroom, then the third room. Still there was no sign of her daughter. She called out again to Beth as she entered the living room. The open floor plan provided her with a good view of the dining area through to the kitchen. The back door stood slightly ajar.

"Beth!" Haley ran to the door and flung it back. The door bounced off the wall. Without slowing down, she ran down the three steps and promptly tripped over her daughter's huddled body. She landed in a heap next to her.

"Hey, Mom," Beth greeted her with a bright smile, still on all fours.

"What are you doing?" Haley placed a hand over her chest to calm herself. Her heart had to have jumped into her throat. Plus she felt as if she were about to pop a lung in an effort to catch her breath. She stood, brushing off pieces of grass and dirt from her robe.

"I'm waiting for the man to come out."

"Man! What man? Here?" Haley pulled up Beth by her arm. She scanned the area, expecting a stranger to lunge at them.

"Relax. He's our landlord."

"Where is he?" Haley continued to look around the enclosed yard. She didn't see anyone.

She wondered whether she should call the police. Someone might not have known that the house was now occupied. The thought of a man wandering around her yard unnerved her. Obviously her daughter needed another chat about talking to strangers. Why on earth didn't she come get her?

"In the shed." Beth pointed to a dilapidated structure off to the side of the property.

"Why is he in the storage shed?"

"He was looking for a lawn mower, but then we thought we heard kittens meowing."

"How long have you been out here?" Haley frowned. It bothered her that she hadn't heard any of this, especially since her bedroom faced the back of the house.

Beth shrugged.

Haley stared at the door, waiting for this mysterious man to emerge. She had rented the property from a management company and had only met the company's representative when she'd come for a visit. It never crossed her mind that she would actually meet the landlord, if that's who was really in the shed.

She picked up a rake and lowered it into position so she could ram the offender. Taking small careful steps, she moved toward the doorway. She looked over her shoulder to tell Beth to stay back. Her daughter stood with her hands folded across her chest, rolling her eyes.

A few more steps and Haley stood directly in front of the shed door. She heard a muted thump, followed by a clatter of tools. There was a muffled grunt and then a colorful swear word. She tightened her hold on the rake and advanced.

The door swung open and a man staggered out holding the side of his head. His T-shirt had dark brown stains with a large rip on one side. His black pants were intact, but wouldn't be considered casual, at least not for rooting around in a dirty shed.

"Who're you?" he asked through gritted teeth. His expression was grim as he continued to press the side of his head.

"I think that I should be asking you that

question." Haley tightened her grip on the rake, aiming it for his midsection. *Hit hard and then run.*

"I'm the landlord. Pierce Masterson." He removed his hand from his head and wiped his palm against his pants leg before offering it to her.

She looked at his dirt-smeared hand and then at his face, focusing on his eyes for any sign that he'd lied. He didn't shift away his gaze or act unsure. She transferred the rake to her other hand and shook his. "Haley Sanders, tenant."

He nodded. "I met Beth earlier. She thought that she'd heard cats, but I don't see any." He looked down at his shirt and brushed at the stains.

The action didn't help, but at least it showed that he wasn't comfortable looking…dirty.

"Do you need to clean up a bit? How about a bag of ice?" Haley tilted her head toward the house, but wasn't sure that she wanted this character in her home.

"Nope. I have a clean shirt in my car. I'll change. I only came over to see if the lawn mower still worked." He touched the small bump that now had formed on his temple. "Unfortunately, with the pile of junk that's in the shed, I couldn't tell."

"Does this mean that I'll have to buy a lawn mower?"

Even though she had relocated without the benefit of a moving company, it had still cost a pretty penny. She'd refused alimony from Vernon, instead instituting a legal order for the money to be placed in trust for their daughter, including the required child support. With a tight budget, she couldn't afford any major expenses until she began working.

"A new mower will be bought," Masterson replied.

"Don't go cheap on it. I know the games owners can play." This man would know that he wasn't dealing with a weak-minded ninny.

He hesitated, but said nothing.

"Whew, it's getting hot out here already. Care for some water? I know that I do." She let him lead the way. Better to keep him in her sights. Walking behind him, she wondered what kind of man would wear dress slacks and loafers to do yard work. Maybe the outfit was for her benefit, knowing that he'd meet his newest tenants.

"I'm going to change and I'll be back," Masterson said over his shoulder. "I have a list of items that I need to fix."

Haley watched him go out the backyard and head to his car. She watched as he strode to a sleek black car buffed to a blinding sheen. It seemed to be on the pricey side for a mere landlord who couldn't afford a handyman. Masterson sat in the driver's seat and pulled off his T-shirt.

The car door prevented a full view, but it couldn't hide everything. It certainly didn't prevent her from seeing a muscular shoulder and chest, the color of brown sugar. Mowing lawns agreed with him. It wasn't just his body, but a handsome profile that acted as an introduction to the potentially fantastic total package. For the first time, she looked forward to her single status.

"Mom?"

"Hmm."

"The kitchen sink is clogged." Beth leaned against the screen door.

Haley turned away as Pierce slipped on a clean shirt. Show over. Reality kicked in with a painful reminder that she might be in over her head now that she was a future home owner.

"I'll get Mr. Masterson to look at it," Beth suggested.

"Sure." Haley didn't hold much stock in the landlord's help. He wasn't bad to look at, but she wasn't sure about his maintenance skills.

The clothes, man and car didn't equal her notion of a handyman.

In the meantime, while he continued to get himself together in the car, she'd go look under the kitchen sink to see what was there.

She found a plunger. For the next five minutes, she tried loosening the clog. The back door swung open and then closed. She didn't have to look up to feel his presence.

"Here, let me have a go."

"I think that I have it, Mr. Masterson."

"Call me Pierce. Too formal otherwise." He watched her fight with the sink. "If you'd let me, I'll snake the line."

"Snake the what?"

"I have this device that I can put down the hole. It won't take long."

Haley stepped away, not really confident that he knew what he was doing. "I'll be right over here. I'm going to make breakfast."

"Already ate," Beth said. "Can I ride my bike?"

"What did you eat?" Haley didn't see any dirty dishes.

"Cereal." Beth headed out the door.

"Not so fast. You don't even know where you're going."

"I'm not going far. Promise." Beth popped a quick peck on her cheek and ran out the door.

Haley stared after her daughter. She didn't want to air their differences in front of this stranger. But at some point, she really had to have a talk with Beth and reset a few rules.

Pierce had the sink operating in no time. He looked out the window over the sink and watched Beth jump on her bike and ride along the side of the house toward the street. Her mother didn't move, but he saw the worry creep and settle like a shadow over her face.

"I'm not going to lie and say that our city is crime free, but it is safer than most," he offered as reassurance.

"That was the major selling point for me."

"It wasn't this wonderful house?" he teased.

"I only saw it once. Lemonade?"

Pierce nodded. She poured his serving into a large glass with lots of ice and a lemon slice. "Thanks, Mrs. Sanders."

"Haley," she said. "How long have you been doing this?"

"Not long, but I've fixed my house and my sisters'."

"Maybe I should call them for references." She sipped her lemonade.

As she held the glass, the diamond encrusted band on her left hand winked at him. The property-management company had told him that it was a mother and her child. No mention made of a husband.

The only reason that he lingered to talk to Haley instead of working was that he was more than mildly interested in Haley Sanders. But the ring ended any further thoughts in that area. Maybe she'd recently married before moving into the house.

He gathered up his tools. "Better get to work before Mr. Sanders comes down and thinks that I'm lollygagging."

"Pierce…is it? I'm the only one that will think you're lollygagging." She set down her glass with a sharp rap on the counter.

He'd made her mad. Was it the husband reference? Was she married? She neither confirmed nor denied her status. Or, was she like Sheena? Was she mad that he didn't think she was in charge?

"What are you thinking?" She folded her arms, still staring at him.

"I'm thinking that you have interesting eyes. They are hazel, but not quite."

"I've heard it all. I have cat eyes that make me look spooky." She rolled her eyes and turned so that he could no longer see her face.

"It's not spooky. Your eyes are beautiful and very unusual." He didn't realize he had moved until he stood next to her. "It'd be a painter's dream to capture their gold and brown color with green flecks."

"Are you an artist, Pierce?" She had the dish towel clutched to her chest.

"I've dabbled." He hadn't painted in years. As he'd grown older, he had pushed it, along with other activities, into the archives of his adolescent obsessions.

She busied herself with the day's meal, moving back and forth between the refrigerator and the counter where he stood. Her looks caught his attention, but he wasn't the type to fall for surface veneer. Haley possessed an intangible quality that had drawn his respect from their initial meeting outside. When she'd stood her ground with a rake pointed at him, he'd seen strength and determination. She was a woman with kick-ass attitude.

"Show me your work one day."

"I'll have to blow off the dust." Was there any law against pursuing a tenant? Wasn't as if she were an employee. Of course, she could complain to the property-management company. That would be embarrassing.

"You always seem to be pondering something."

He contemplated answering her.

"Spit it out," she demanded. "Are you a brooder? Walking around with your hands behind your back, pondering the world's problems?"

"Since you put it that way, I had two things on my mind. Would you be offended if I asked you out? And the other question, which keeps nagging at me, is whether you're married or not?" Pierce would've loved to ask those questions with his face hidden behind the Sunday papers. He determined that Haley, however, needed to see his sincerity. He needed to assure her that he wasn't a man from the mean streets trying to get fresh.

"That answer was much more than I expected."

Pierce knew he'd blindsided her. The effect caused her to move around the kitchen, wiping the counter and then pausing to look at him before resuming the task. "Looks like it's my turn to ask what you're thinking."

"Haven't dated in years. Not sure if I can handle the thought of a date right now."

He hoped that he hid his disappointment well.

"What if we don't call it a date?" she suggested. "I know you didn't use that word. But I don't want it hanging over me. It'll remind me that there are dating rules, including all that pre- and post-dating do's and don'ts." She shuddered. "I may have to look at a popular sitcom to know what's acceptable."

Pierce joined Haley's laughter. He liked that she didn't appear to mind poking fun at herself.

"If I check on you, Pierce Masterson, will I find out that you ask out your other tenants?"

"You won't find out much. I don't take much time to do such things." He didn't even have one serious relationship in his past. No woman had gotten that close.

"Let's have after-dinner coffee, then. Wednesday at seven? You name the place," Haley counteroffered.

Pierce provided the name and directions for Haley. He wanted to grin and pump his fist, happy that he and Haley shared a mutual attraction. "I need to get back to work." He drained his glass. "Here's the list of things I need to do in this house." She took the list from him, reviewed it and handed it back to him.

"Are you doing all of this today? Seems to be quite a bit."

"I'll have to work it into my schedule. These projects should take about a week."

"Let me know when you'll need to get into my bedroom. I'll be sure to clean up so you won't judge me." She chuckled.

"Will do." He headed outside to fix the first step at the bottom of the back door. He pushed open the screen door.

"By the way, Pierce, my ex-husband is very much a matter of the past. The ring helps me in certain situations, if you know what I mean."

"I understand completely."

Pierce usually looked forward to the weekend. Friday was game night at Sheena's. Sheena, her husband, Carlton Sr., Laura and he played various board games, trivia games, anything that fed their competitive spirits. Saturday night was usually spent looking at sports on television, depending on the season. Then Sunday was family dinner, where all the siblings met at Sheena's.

Often, Omar canceled on dinner because he had

a date. No one pressed him to bring his date, figuring that if he didn't initiate that suggestion, then his companion wasn't worth the family introduction.

Part of the family-night ritual included Pierce picking up Laura on the way to Sheena's. His sister didn't have too many dates to conflict. Sheena had accused him of scaring the men away. He called it protecting his little sister from potential creeps. Laura's sweet nature reminded him of their mother. She'd had a forgiving attitude that hadn't always worked to her advantage.

This Sunday evening, he had no messages on his answering machine. With the weekend almost over, only one call interested him. Sheena hadn't called him. She couldn't possibly be serious about not talking to him.

Sitting at home in front of his laptop playing solitare made him feel like a loser. No girlfriends to call in a pinch. No real buddies who were living the partying bachelor life. And now, no family to call and hang out with.

After the computer beat him for the umpteenth time and his nacho chips and salsa supply were depleted, he flopped down on his couch uttering a loud curse.

"What the heck, I'm going to do it," he muttered. An idea had formed and he wanted to clap himself on the back for thinking of it. He drove to Laura's townhome around the same time that he always picked her up. He pulled up in front of the gated community of condos and punched in the code that his sister had shared with him. In no time he'd parked and now knocked on the door.

"Hi, Pierce." Laura hugged him briefly in the doorway.

"Hey, Laura, you ready?" He noticed that she didn't move away from the doorway, nor did she invite him in.

They exchanged pleasantries as he remained standing in the hallway. He expected Sheena to act in this manner, not Laura, his usual ally.

"Are you going to let me in?"

"I really wish that I could. Sheena and I agreed that it's best if we keep our distance from you for a little while." She wrung her hands as if delivering the news depleted all her energy.

"Those are Sheena's words, not yours. And may I remind you that you agreed with my decision."

"I went along with it, but that doesn't necessarily mean that I agreed with it."

"Since when did you get so sneaky?" The one person he could rely on had switched sides.

His younger sister stared back at him, unfazed by his anger and accusation. She was also light complected like Sheena, but dressed quieter, without the loud colors and crazy designs. Her clothes tended to be muted shades of charcoal, grays and lots of black. Her only makeup was a touch of gloss to her lips, while her hair was either pulled back with a ponytail holder or twisted in a bun with hair clips.

Unlike Sheena, she was so un-diva-like. He constantly complimented her about this wonderful trait because she didn't play power games. Now his pure, sweet Laura had been corrupted.

"You're going to dis me, too," he stated the obvious.

"Please don't look at it that way. We simply feel that you didn't fully engage us in the discussion and decision. You're the head and we're the body. One can't move without the other. I think that you forgot that point." She took him back to his school days at St. John's Catholic School when he'd often been scolded by the nuns.

A car horn sounded.

"My ride is here." Laura eased out of the

condo, forcing him to step farther back into the hallway. "Let me know when you want to have another family meeting. Here's my two cents' advice. I think that you'll need to have the discussion at a different place, Sheena's or mine. Your attitude doesn't go over well when you play lord of the manor in your home." She hugged him, patted his cheek and walked down the hall.

He hurried past her. He'd bet anything that Sheena waited for her downstairs. This had gone too far. Now his older sister was pulling a queen-bee routine on him.

He ran out of the building, heading straight to Sheena's car. The tinted window rolled down. Instead of Sheena, her husband looked back at him.

"Where's your crazy wife?"

"At home preparing dinner."

"Are you in on this, too?" Carlton wasn't his favorite in-law, although he was the only one. He'd never done anything to disrespect his sister. But Pierce knew that one day this man would screw up and then he would be waiting for him.

"I do as I'm told. Sheena said go get Laura. I put down my remote and I came to get her."

Pierce glared at him. This behavior was his problem. He needed to stand up to Sheena. Since

Carlton obviously didn't have the fortitude, then it was up to him.

And darn it, he was hungry for a home-cooked meal.

Laura got into the front seat. Pierce grabbed the back door to jump in. The door was locked.

"I don't think that you'll want to come to dinner to make a scene," Laura told him through the open window. "Sheena invited the pastor and his wife."

Pierce thought about the possibility, then dropped his hand. "Nice touch," he muttered, recognizing that he'd lost this round.

The car pulled away with his sister waving at him. All of this nonsense over a house. Why couldn't they accept what he'd told them? Even if he gave in and had the family discussion, he'd already committed to Haley that he would sell.

She needed the house.

All he had to do was convince them that she was the ideal candidate, as he had already concluded. And he had to accomplish this small feat without alerting Haley that the house was a source of conflict. Thank goodness she had agreed to go out with him.

He sighed and walked back to his car. It would have to be Chinese takeout for dinner.

Chapter 3

Haley fussed in the mirror. She couldn't get the right side of her hairstyle to curl properly. In a last-ditch effort, she applied the curling iron to tame its wayward flip.

"Mom, quit it." Beth took the comb from her hands and fixed the hair with her fingers. "All done."

"I'm only going for coffee and I'll be right back."

"I'm a big girl. Plus you lectured me to death about opening the back door. Don't want to have that experience again." Beth did an exaggerated shudder.

Haley made a face at her daughter. "I'm not trying to be a nag. And I really won't stay long."

"Especially if you don't leave in the next five minutes."

Haley shot up, still doing a last-minute inspection of her image. "Should I wear the mules or the flip-flops?" She'd selected a simple blouse and a pair of slacks. "I don't want Pierce to think that I'm on a date."

Beth rolled her eyes. "Mom, you're so lame. I'd wear the sandals, but considering that you haven't had a pedicure, the mules would be better."

Haley looked at her feet, wiggling her bare toes.

"At least put on the toe ring we bought at the mall."

"I told you that it felt weird."

"Shows that you're hip." Beth held out the tiny band.

Haley took the silver ring and slipped it on her second toe. She didn't see a miraculous transformation, but she'd go along with Beth's recommendation. "Gotta run. I'll call you when I get there and when I'm leaving."

"You're worse than a warden."

"What if I'm doing it for my safety?"

"Fine. Call me every five minutes and especially if he tries to get fresh." Beth puckered up. Haley shot a strong disapproving look, which brought knee-slapping laughter from Beth.

Haley decided to ignore her daughter. Instead she looked over the directions once more and then drove to the coffee shop. To her surprise, when she arrived, the parking lot was filled with cars. College kids spilled out onto the sidewalk where there were a few additional tables. Since when did after-dinner coffee get so popular?

Haley took a deep breath to squelch her nerves before opening the door to the shop. Inside, it reminded her of the lounge areas in her college dorm. Thick, comfy chairs and tables populated one part of the shop. A smaller section displayed items for sale. She moved closer to look at the mugs, carafes, even CDs.

"Haley, over here."

Haley spied Pierce at the only table for two near the pickup counter. She returned his wave and hurried over.

"Have you been waiting long?" she asked.

"I came a little early because I knew that getting a table could be a pain."

"Didn't realize that this was such a popular thing."

"Gourmet coffee cafés are big. Take a look at the menu board and I'll order."

"Thanks, but we're going dutch. Remember, this isn't a date."

"Right, I forgot." He grinned. "You go ahead, I'll hold the table."

Haley looked at the various flavors, not sure what to order. Since Pierce wasn't standing beside her to give a quick orientation, she now stood in front of the cashier drawing a mental blank. "I'll try the iced mango-flavored green tea." She turned down the dessert offers of cakes, cookies, scones.

Soon it was Pierce's turn. Haley waited until he returned before trying her tea.

"Did you want to share my chocolate marble cake?" Pierce cut his slice into two pieces and slid half to her on a napkin.

"No, thanks. Looks delicious, but I have to watch my weight."

"Take my word for it. You're not overweight. Not even close." He bit into his piece. "Women worry about weight and body fat too much."

"Easy for you to say." She envied how he ate

his slice without agonizing about the calories and the fat content. "Do you exercise?"

"I do an hour every day. I'm no role model, though. I skip meals on a regular basis."

Haley looked at his hands. His fingers were long and tapered. She didn't see any calluses, although the fleshy side of his palm was covered by a Band-Aid. "What happened?"

"The hammer got too close to my hand and I pinched it between two pieces of wood."

"Ouch." Haley grimaced at the thought. "Why don't you hire someone?"

"I had that exact thought when the pain rang through my hand to my head. If I do get someone, then I won't get a chance to see you as often."

Haley grabbed the piece of cake and bit into it. She didn't know how to respond. Having someone interested in her seemed strange. Her ex-husband used to be the only person to comment on her attractiveness. In his estimation, her looks had faded.

"Hey, don't get quiet on me." Pierce touched her softly on her wrist.

"It's not you. Like I said, it's been a while. I don't know what to say. I'm thinking too much or maybe, not enough. It's been only three days since I've moved in and I'm out with a man."

"And he's asked you to marry him."

"What?"

"Well, I figured that's what your mind will come up with for the next installment," he teased.

"See, this isn't good. You're a mind reader."

"Have two sisters who are completely opposite. But they give me a good sample of what's important to women."

"Sounds like you don't get away with much," Haley laughed. "Maybe I should thank your sisters for their efforts."

"And maybe you shouldn't." Pierce's brow furrowed in mock outrage. "I know how to treat my date."

"Not that we're on a date, but for conversation sake, how would you treat a date?" Haley licked her lips, her mouth felt dry.

Pierce moved his drink out of the way and balled up the used tissue. Then he slid his hand under hers so that hers lightly rested on top. Haley hesitated. Should she stare at her hands that tingled at his touch? Or should she return his steady gaze?

"I think a man should be chivalrous. But I also think that he should be comfortable with his date taking the lead on what is appropriate."

"Appropriate? Like holding hands," Haley prompted.

"Or sharing a kiss," he offered.

She barely heard his voice over the enthusiastic chatter surrounding them. But the word kiss sounded as if he'd yelled it at her. In that instant, she couldn't stop looking at his lips, thinking about how they'd feel pressed against hers. *Whoa! Where did that come from?*

Haley pulled her hand away from Pierce. She didn't want to raise his expectation, yet her body was giving off signals for a lot more than she was willing to handle.

Conversation dragged, regardless of Pierce's attempt to lighten the change in mood. Haley wanted to retreat to her home. She hoped that he'd allow her to take the lead, as he'd stated, to conclude their meeting. She finished her drink and quickly made her excuse to leave.

There was no way that she was ready to deal with a man, not even a drop-dead gorgeous hunk.

Haley conceded that everything in her life didn't fit into a neat cubbyhole. Her daughter hadn't fallen in love with her new school. Pretending that she could handle a coffee shop meeting with a man only revealed how unprepared she was to deal with that part of her life. Now her job presented its own complexities, but she couldn't run away from her only source of income.

Two months under Haley's belt as an events coordinator for the city's convention center did little to calm her jitters. If she'd been a nail-biter, she would've gnawed her way to the cuticle. It wasn't every day that a former housewife sat across from a bank owner and his designer-suited entourage of advisers to discuss business. She awaited his decision. All she had to accomplish was his acceptance of their bid to host the community bank's annual meeting. Her first major deal would serve as insurance for remaining employed.

The advisers hovered over the paperwork. The all-male ensemble spoke in hushed tones, never making eye contact with her. The silver-haired owner merely sat back in the thick leather overstuffed chair with his hands steepled over his ample chest.

He, at least, acknowledged her. They'd talked about the warm spring weather, the influx of retirees to the area and the need for a gourmet coffeehouse on Main Street.

But she was no fool. This was a shrewd man. Although she'd presented her spiel on Hampton Mews, she didn't think that the test was over. And that brought on the familiar heartburn symptoms.

"I have a few reservations that you'll need to address."

The advisers stopped their huddle and fixed their attention on their boss. They resembled hummingbirds hovering on the verge of taking off in whatever direction he commanded. Anticipation hung heavily over the group as they followed their boss's line of sight toward her.

Nothing like a little pressure.

"I assure you that the city's infrastructure can handle five hundred attendees. We hosted the regional high-school basketball tournament last year. We were able to handle that event without any problems," she said. "Five hundred people. Yep, that should be fine. It should be…I think it will be…fine," she finished with a false perkiness. She'd have to get on the phone and contract out many of the details to pull off the event, but Mr. Thadeus Bedford didn't have to know that.

He leaned forward in the chair. He didn't take

his eyes off her. Then he took a deep breath and exhaled. "I hope so. This is a major anniversary for the company. And I am not partial to small towns, but my staff here kept talking about Golden Spring." He sniffed as if the air wasn't up to his standard, either. "Although, I must say, your award-winning golf courses did appeal to me."

Guess that was his way of saying that she couldn't take credit for her presentation getting his interest in the town. Haley pasted on a smile. *It's all about the customer. Treat him with courtesy.* "That's very gracious of you. I'll pass on your comments to the golf-course owner." *Focus on their needs.* "And for those who may not be golf enthusiasts, our two major hotel chains do have celebrity revues and Vegas-style casinos."

Bedford sniffed. Again his nose aimed a little higher, while his lips turned down a little lower. He cleared his throat. She now connected the sound with his displeasure.

A sharp knock on the conference-room door interrupted her pitch. Vera, her assistant, popped her head into the room. "Sorry to disturb you, Ms. Sanders. You have an important call on line one."

Haley needed an interruption, but not that. She

stared at Vera, hoping she'd understand the silent message to retreat.

Vera didn't.

"Please take a message." Haley delivered her request with as much sweetness as she could manage.

Instead of leaving, Vera stepped farther into the room.

Haley cringed. Her fashion-challenged assistant sported a bright pink pantsuit with a sunny-yellow scarf and white tennis shoes. To top it off, a country-western singer, big-hair look framed her face with massive upward flips.

Great. Bedford couldn't get a deeper groove along his forehead if he tried. Irritation practically crackled from his large frame.

"Well…it's Dr. Masterson," Vera offered.

A doctor? Since she'd come to town, Haley had only gone to a doctor once. Actually she'd taken her daughter, Beth, for her physical in order to enroll her into school. But that had been several months ago and she didn't recall any Dr. Masterson. The only Masterson who came to mind was Pierce Masterson, her landlord. What were the chances that her landlord was related to a doctor?

In a small town, it could be possible. Haley gnawed at her lip. Why the games? Unless...

Nope. She'd reserve judgment until she got to her office. Her mouth tightened. Like a gentle breeze rustling dried leaves, her anger stirred. Did he think that playing the landlord and coming to her house would give him an in with her?

She realized that if she'd not gotten cold feet on their date, she'd have learned more about Pierce. Maybe he would have told her. Her anger settled into unease.

"Vera, is it Beth?" A sickening dread dropped like a boulder in her gut.

Vera nodded.

Haley turned her attention back to the group. All eyes were focused on her.

"Is everything okay?" Bedford asked.

Haley nodded, but struggled to push back the panic simmering under the surface. She waved Vera away. "Take down the information, please."

She turned her attention to Bedford and tried to smile, but her lips trembled. Next would come the tears. She swallowed. *Don't break down in front of the potential clients.*

"My apologies, gentlemen, let's get back to the business at hand."

"I do not rush to my decisions, Ms. Sanders. It's my policy to sleep in the town and try out the amenities. Then I will make my decision. Let's meet in two days." For the first time, Bedford smiled. "And now, you're needed elsewhere."

"Thank you." Maybe he wasn't as fierce as his reputation purported.

"Ten in the morning on Thursday."

"You're staying at the Windsor, right?" When he nodded, she continued, "I'll be in the lounge."

"Until then, good day." Bedford and his small entourage left the room. Her boss magically appeared on cue to escort them to the exit.

Haley didn't waste another minute. There was no time to dissect how she should've closed the deal. She couldn't ponder what her boss would say under the guise of constructive criticism. Or whether she successfully could make it through her six-month probation without this deal.

Please don't let anything be wrong with Beth, she prayed. But something had to be wrong for the call. A sob choked her as she ran through the hall to her office. She had to be strong. Nothing could happen to her little girl. Her daughter was her life. She grabbed her car keys and headed to Vera's desk to pick up the contact information.

Not until she sat in the car did she look down at the memo. *Dr. Masterson wants to discuss a serious matter. He has Beth at his office. 20013 Crystal Lane.*

The note didn't indicate that Beth was hurt. However, this bit of insight didn't settle her nerves.

Ten minutes later, Haley pulled into the diagonal parking spaces in front of the doctor's office in the medical park. As she got out, she noticed that her car straddled the thick white lines. Another day she would've gotten back into her car and made the necessary adjustment to avoid offending another driver.

Not today. She ran the few yards to the door, her pulse beating erratically.

She burst into the office and headed for the receptionist's desk. "Is Beth here? I'm here to see Dr. Masterson. I'm Beth's mother." The words tumbled out in a gasp. Her chest heaved from the exertion. Her hands shook as she pushed her hair away from her face.

"Ms. Sanders, in here please."

Haley looked up when she heard a familiar deep voice.

Pierce stood at the doorway separating the reception area and the examination rooms. The first thing she noticed was his thick eyebrows underlining a deep frown. They sat like black accent marks over intense brown eyes framed by those enviable long lashes. He didn't smile in friendly greeting.

Neither did she.

"What game are you playing?" She marched right up to him and placed her hand on her hip. "You're a doctor," she accused. Her anger took on tornado-size proportions, escalating through her body and looking for a place to touch down. In Pierce's face seemed like a good place for an explanation.

To think that she had been attracted by his easy, down-home manner. It didn't help that his ruggedly handsome features had stirred up her imagination, causing her to blush to the roots of her hair.

"Let's go to my office, shall we?"

"Does this mean that Beth is not sick or hurt?" Haley looked around, making sure to look in any rooms that were open. She wasn't prepared yet to see her daughter lying on an examination table heavily bandaged, profusely bleeding.

"Not hardly." His clipped tone sent a warning

that this might not be the type of doctor visit that she originally thought it'd be.

It became clear that Beth wasn't on her way to the emergency room, but in trouble of another kind. Haley lengthened her footsteps to keep up with Pierce's march to his office. Since he wasn't talking, she felt compelled to stay quiet.

She felt as if she were meeting Pierce for the first time. He walked like a man in charge with his shoulders back and spine ramrod straight. His white coat barely moved with impressive efficiency. He wore casual khaki slacks perfectly creased.

She had pretty much kept their relationship to the landlord-tenant conditions on the lease agreement. She'd taken that hard-and-fast route in order not to succumb to her urges to get closer to him, to occasionally share a glass of wine with him on the back porch steps while watching the sunset. With his list of items to be fixed or replaced completed, she hadn't seen him in over a month.

Pierce stopped in front of an office door bearing his name. He stepped aside, bidding her entry. "Have a seat, Haley."

She stepped in, surprised at the small space.

Considering his autocratic air, she'd expected an office that encompassed the width of the property. Instead, the room contained only the necessities with a desk, side table for the computer and a bookcase filled to capacity. It barely had room for two extra chairs, efficient without pomp and circumstance. She looked up at him, waiting for him to clear up all the questions that buzzed around in her head.

"Beth is fine."

Clearly he wasn't. His jaw twitched. Was it Beth or her that made him look as if he'd rather be dealing with his patients?

He took his seat behind the desk. "I'm concerned about Beth. She made a poor decision today. I presume that she's about thirteen or fourteen years old and should understand the consequences of bad judgment."

He was being so formal with her. His words, his tone, the dour expression judged her on his turf. "Pierce. Dr. Masterson, please tell me, what's going on? And for the record, my daughter is thirteen."

He tapped a rhythm on the desk, staring at her.

"Look, Pierce, you said this was an emergency." She fidgeted, smoothing her skirt, brushing away nonexistent lint. "Where's my daughter?" She stood and headed into the hallway.

"This way." He led her down the hallway toward the lit exit sign and eventual door.

Haley hesitantly walked out the door, looking up at him for an explanation. Why were they standing outside behind his office?

"Take a look at the back wall."

Haley walked to the end of the building and turned. "Oh my! What is this?"

"The better question is who did this?"

Haley saw Beth and another woman, who looked as if she was one of Pierce's employees, dressed in a medical uniform, chatting. Beth sat cross-legged on the ground chewing gum and blowing bubbles, animatedly talking as if nothing were terribly wrong.

"Beth, would you tell your mother why I had to call her?"

"You…she did this?"

"For some reason your daughter felt that this concrete fencing was a huge canvas for her and her friends. The friends ran off, leaving her holding the bag."

"I wasn't trying to run away, Dr. Masterson," Beth defended with teenage attitude. She wore an admiring smile as she sauntered over to the wall. "I'd say that we brightened this wall."

"Why did you pick my wall?"

"Because I know you. I wouldn't put in all this work to make a stranger's place look good."

"I don't think my patients will care for the graffiti. And might I add that my landlord and the other businesses in the area would have a fit."

"Mom!"

"Bethany Lindsey Sanders, don't say another word, young lady. What were you thinking? You know better. I can't believe you let your so-called friends talk you into acting like a delinquent."

"You don't know my friends. I don't talk about your friends. Dr. Masterson has old people for his patients. And just because they are old doesn't mean that they don't like bright colors or pretty things."

"Don't give me lip, girl!"

Beth's response was to focus on the dirt patterns she made with her toe.

Haley had to remember this wasn't about her. This wasn't about how embarrassed she was at this minute. Nor was it about what the neighbors would say.

She was the mother and her daughter had to

remember that she was not a one-person demolition unit. Vernon had been the disciplinarian; even immediately after the divorce, he'd stepped in whether she'd wanted him to do so or not. Being a single parent was akin to playing an octopus; unfortunately, Haley hadn't sprouted the other six hands to cope.

"Can we work something out?" Haley opened her pocketbook.

"That won't do."

"I'm willing to pay." Good grief. Was Pierce going to play hardball with her? "I hope this isn't about me…you know…not continuing to go out with you."

"I'm not a sixteen-year-old getting over a crush."

"Sorry. Well, that certainly put me in my place." She offered a tight, fake smile. "Could you tell me how much to write the check?" Her pen was poised over the line printed on the check. Beth wasn't going to see the light of day anytime soon. "Stop chewing that gum before I plug your nose with it."

Beth had the good grace to look shocked and promptly spat the gum onto Pierce's shoe.

"I don't want money." Pierce shook his foot until the gum was dislodged.

Haley looked at the extent of the damage to the wall. She couldn't imagine the cost or the dent this check would make in her already low account.

"I'm demanding hard labor and…"

"What hard labor?"

"Beth has to repaint the wall before my landlord slaps me with damages."

Haley wanted to sag with relief. She nodded her agreement at the light and inexpensive punishment.

"You want me to paint the entire wall by myself?" Beth asked incredulously and looked at Haley for support.

"You're not only going to paint the wall. You will also get several tasks that you have to complete each day at home. I'm killing myself going to work and then coming home to do more work. Obviously you have too much time on your hands. Since you want to act as if you don't have any common sense, I will treat you as such until you prove otherwise."

Beth's mouth trembled. Her fists balled. Haley knew that she and Beth were getting off easy. She also feared that Beth was on the verge of a meltdown. Haley decided to continue this in the privacy of her home. "Pierce, please give me a call to work out the details."

"Sure."

"And thanks." She offered him her hand. He shook it, holding it until she looked up in his face.

Pierce wished that she could trust him enough to be friends. He'd tell her how much he approved of her firm stance. He'd also tell her that he hadn't been able to think of anything else but their two non-dates. He'd apologize for whatever he'd said or done to spook her. Goodness knows, he missed those beautiful eyes that made him feel as if he had fallen backward into a pool only to sink to its depth with a silly smile on his face.

By trade, he fixed bodies gone awry. Working with elderly patients, he saw the frustration in their eyes when their bodies limited their actions. He took pride in closing the gap between what they wanted to do and what they were capable of doing.

He hadn't spent enough time with Beth and her mother to know how to fix them. But he was quite certain that something was broken.

"I have another solution," he offered. He walked toward the wall and studied its length.

"Yes?" He jumped at Beth's voice. He had

been so taken in with the scene that he hadn't heard her approach.

He looked down into the young teen's face squinting up at him. Amazing how adolescent emotions can rage in one minute and be soft and innocent in another. "I have an idea. I won't pursue the matter if Beth agrees to volunteer once a week to bring her talent into the office. Maybe she could do a mural on one the walls in the waiting room. Of course, I and the rest of the staff would have to approve it." He faced Haley, unsure why she looked so doubtful.

"Shut up! No. You've got to be kidding." Beth snorted.

Thankfully he'd heard that "shut up" expression from his patients' grandchildren to know it was the latest cool thing to say. He wondered if the first child who'd said it was now toothless.

"Oh man! How long do I have?" Beth's face transformed.

"How about getting it done by the end of the month? Then I can have a festival open-house sort of thing and unveil your work."

"You've got a deal."

"I'm not sure." Haley stared at him.

"What's the problem?" He didn't expect her to

whoop and holler around the parking lot like her daughter. But he definitely didn't expect the suspicious glint in her eyes.

She pulled him aside while Beth continued to dance around the lot. "Your office, please. I think you should've discussed it with me, first."

"What is there to discuss? I think this is the best solution." He followed her to his office where she slammed the door shut.

"I'd much rather have the fence repainted and leave it at that."

"But that's not what I want. Beth needs to take responsibility, but I think giving her options to express her emotions will help stabilize her." Why couldn't she trust him to know what was right?

"Pierce, I appreciate your generosity, but as Beth's parent I determine what's best for her."

"Duly noted. I was merely following the philosophy that it takes a village. Hampton Mews isn't a village, but it still has a small-town appeal. Everyone knows everyone. We like to help each other. Haley, I'm not the enemy."

"You're not my friend, either."

"Not by choice. You have a fence all of your own that you've managed to erect in record time."

"You said this wasn't about me."

"I lied." He leaned against his desk. "I didn't plan for Beth to play Leonardo on my wall. It happened. I think that I can truly help her because I'm sure that it's difficult for her to handle all these adjustments in her life. Plus I think the girl has talent."

"And that's why we can't continue to go out. I can't add us to one of her adjustments."

"To argue with you would make me sound as if I'm not considerate of your daughter's feelings. That's not true. But I'm also considerate of yours."

"You don't know what I'm feeling, *Doctor.*"

"Why is my being a doctor bothering you? I didn't lie. It didn't come up. I would've loved to share that with you, but you didn't give me a chance. Shouldn't the fact that I'm gainfully employed sway you to my side?" he questioned, his eyebrows raised in question.

"I'm not answering any of your questions. Where's Beth?"

"She's out back. I'm sure she's appreciating my attempts to delay you. Would you let me appear to have success?"

Pierce watched Haley's mouth open, then snap shut. She turned from him toward the door, then stopped. Her eyes narrowed. She approached him. "You're giving me a heart attack," she said, but a small smile tugged at her mouth.

He put his stethoscope in his ears and closed the gap between them to mere inches. "May I?"

She responded with a smile.

He placed the device on her chest and listened to her heart. He closed his eyes, noting the heart-beats increasing. He heard the whisper of her breath, feeling it brush his neck.

"What do you hear, Doctor? Have I passed the physical?"

"I'd like to check one more thing before handing you a prescription." He pulled open his desk drawer and retrieved a pad of blank pre-scription forms. He quickly wrote the remedy and folded the paper.

She reached for it.

"I need to complete the exam."

"Pierce." She placed a hand on his chest.

He waited for Haley to look at him. He wanted to see in her eyes the same desire that he couldn't contain, but had spread through his body like a wildfire out of control. Regardless of what she said, she couldn't continue to deny that they shared emotions that ran intense and deep.

She tiptoed and kissed him softly. He needed no further encouragement before covering her lips.

His tongue stroked her mouth, playing with its fullness, before slipping between her lips. Her hands slid up his back, grabbing and releasing his doctor's gown. He tightened his embrace, afraid that she'd simply vanish in his arms. Everything about her was magical. He desperately didn't want their first kiss to be his last, which is why he had to stop before it was too late.

He kissed her softly before pulling away. His mouth continued to tingle, seeking the sensual warmth of her mouth.

"I can't believe that I did that." She touched her mouth, shifting away eye contact with him.

"I can believe it. Our attraction is beautiful and natural."

"I don't think that I can give you what you want from me. My emotions, any feelings that I would have for another man, any desires are on empty. Have you ever been married?"

He shook his head.

"In the final year, my marriage used me and spit me out. I have nothing to give."

"Don't judge and condemn me for being a man. I'll take whatever you share. And I know that I'll have to open myself to you. You see, you're not the only one whose knees are knocking."

"What's my prescription?"

He handed her the paper and watched her read it. She didn't react, simply refolding it before putting it in her pocketbook.

"I think that I can give you one official date. But with every prescriptive drug, there are side effects. What are the side effects?"

"Strong addiction to continue dating. An increasing desire for more kisses. Spending lazy afternoons with a charming doctor at your side— for medical purposes, of course."

Haley grinned. "Let's go check on Beth."

Chapter 4

Haley couldn't catch her breath. Locking lips with Pierce was like sampling a sugary treat that wakened the senses, but did nothing for calming them down. She replayed the mind-scrambling experience in her mind over and over to feed a burgeoning addiction.

She'd have to put all of that on the back burner. Now was the time to be the stern parent and deal with her child.

The cell phone hanging at her waistband rang. She pulled it off to glance at the telephone number

on the small screen. "Crap!" It was her job. She
didn't want to answer, knowing it wasn't a call to
show concern. The culture in the office didn't lend
itself to warm and fuzzy relations among the employees.

She hadn't had her six-month review yet. This
wasn't the time to mess around with her job. Frustrated, she rapped the phone against her temple.
"Darn it, not now." She brought the phone to her
ear.

Vera, her assistant, told her to hold while she
connected her with Mr. Strayer, the boss. Haley
squeezed her eyes shut, gritting her teeth against
what she was sure would be bad news. So far,
most of her meetings with Mr. Strayer weren't
compliments on a job well done. He took delight
in reiterating their goal to attract businesses to the
city and its amenities.

"Haley," Strayer's voice boomed over the cell
phone. "I need you back in the office right away.
Thadeus Bedford called looking for you. He's
made his decision and will be over in an hour to
discuss the fine points."

"No kidding?" Haley pumped her fist in
victory. "That's great." Haley did a two-step for
landing the big deal. The former housewife with

all her insecurities could stay in the closet a little while longer. "I thought that he was going to do more research before making a decision?"

"Nope. He called and asked if you were back from your emergency. I told him yes, but you were tied up in a meeting. Then he said that he'd arrived at his decision and would be over."

"I'll be right there, Mr. Strayer." She closed the phone and turned to address Beth, only to see Pierce and Beth staring at her.

"What?"

"I thought you'd be taking Beth home."

"Of course I will. Beth understands that I have to go back to work. This is important." She looked from Pierce to Beth and saw her daughter's disappointment that quickly got tucked away behind a mask of indifference.

"Beth." She approached the young girl, who sidestepped her. "I'm asking for your understanding."

"And I'm asking for yours." Beth glared at her and then went back to digging her toe in the dirt.

The back door to the building opened. A woman stuck out her head, her eyes lighting on Pierce. "Dr. Masterson, your schedule is falling behind. We need you in here."

"Looks like I'll have to leave you ladies. I'll be in touch, Haley. Beth, I'm looking forward to seeing what you can do with my reception area."

"Thanks, Doc." Beth offered him a bright, cheery smile. Haley knew that display was for her benefit.

She escorted Beth to her car. She had mounds of guilt that were self-created, requiring her to wade through. Beth's antics didn't help. For the first time, she wondered if Beth would be better off with her father. Her daughter didn't seem to hold him with the contempt that she regularly flashed at her.

No one said it would be easy, either.

A familiar blue car puttered up the street. The brakes screeched, metal grinding against metal, until the car came to a complete stop. The college freshman Haley had hired through a day-care-provider service jumped out of the car and ran toward them. Her small braids framed her head, stopping below the chin. This week the micro plaits were a deep burgundy.

"Miss Haley, I just heard. I waited at the bus stop, but Beth wasn't there. Then I saw some of the other kids walking home in the neighborhood and they told me." She flung a wayward braid away from her eye.

"Everything is fine, Lezlie. Beth got herself into a bit of a mess, though. I'll fill you in later, but I have to run. Can you take her home, please?"

"You're not coming? You said that you would take me home and then leave." Haley cringed from Beth's disappointment.

"Sorry, hon, I won't be coming right now. The sooner that I can get to the meeting, the sooner I can come home."

"You haven't been home until late all this week."

"I'll make it up to you over the weekend." Haley bit her lip. "This is my boss. This is what brings food on the table. Please, let's not fight." In her heart, her daughter always came first. But she needed this job, more precisely this project, to show that she could do the job. Haley put her arm around Beth and walked with her to Lezlie's car. She seemed so thin. Haley uneasily studied her daughter.

"Come on, Beth. I know you've got lots of homework." Lezlie opened her car door while the very reluctant teen scooted in. "Finish up early and I'll make that banana split that you're always bugging me about."

Haley leaned against the passenger side

looking at Beth's profile. "I promise. I'll be home before your favorite TV show is over at eight."

"My favorite show plays on Monday. There's nothing good on television on Tuesdays. And Wednesdays I'm working on my English composition weekly assignment." She spoke to the windshield, not turning to address Haley.

Clearly Beth was letting her know that she didn't have a clue what her evening schedule was like.

"Besides, I might be asleep by the time you come in."

Lezlie pulled off. Neither girl returned Haley's wave.

"Not if I can help it, baby." Haley walked to her car, got in and drove away in the opposite direction. As she drove back to work, Haley reflected on how she had come to this part in her life.

One day she had been the corporate wife hosting lavish parties, dressed in her favorite designer ensemble and facilitating tours of her expertly decorated, mansion-size family home. Without preamble and after fourteen years of marriage, her husband's indiscretions had graduated into an openly adulterous lifestyle, with younger, slimmer and ever perkier partners. The humiliating experience seemed like a clichéd ending to her marriage that could rival television's latest dramas, but it was her nightmarish reality.

Once Vernon got wind of her divorce intentions, he'd cut her off financially. In his screwed-up mind, he expected her to deal with his infidelity since he still took care of their financial needs. Considering that her in-laws shared a similar marital arrangement, she knew better than to take her problems to them.

She'd learned to cope and plan. She'd started banking her shopping allowances from Vernon by making purchases, then bringing them home for him to see. A few days later, she'd returned the merchandise for the cash. She'd saved in this way until she could afford a divorce lawyer.

The only bright spot in her wretched divorce had come when the judge awarded her full custody of Beth.

After the divorce, their mutual friends had treated Haley as an outcast, especially once she moved out of their exclusive neighborhood. She'd never been close to her in-laws, who thought she was common and lacking in the social graces. And she had quickly tired of Vernon's sudden appearances to see Beth, despite the set visitation schedule. She'd wanted to start fresh and rebuild her life on her own terms.

Hampton Mews hadn't been an urban mecca, but it offered a sense of normalcy in her chaotic life. The city had been featured in the newspaper in the top five emerging cities with low crime rate, good schools and low housing costs. The community's only downside was the local job situation. Most people commuted an hour by car to Frederick or Baltimore to work. She'd been lucky enough to be in the right place at the right time when she'd landed her job.

The spirit of this city spoke to her soul. Even its location nestled between two mountain ranges had a natural shield against the elements. It was a place of new beginnings and putting down roots.

Pierce tried hard to fit in all his remaining patients that afternoon. Luckily his receptionist had had the foresight and nerve to force him into reality and to call him back into the office. She'd rescheduled three patients with his sincerest regrets.

Now that it was summer, he'd have to show up at barbeques, family dinners, grandchildren's baptisms and flea-market bazaars for redemption. He couldn't complain. Working as a doctor in the field of geriatrics had always been his dream. When his father had left, he'd tried, but couldn't always handle all the responsibilities as the man in charge. Senior members of the neighborhood had watched over him and helped him. Other families' fathers and grandfathers had taught him to be a man and how to take care of his family.

Long hours and constant training had now earned him the distinction of being a leading doctor in senior care. It still took years to earn his patients' trust. He didn't ever want to take their faith in him for granted.

Breaking out of his reverie, Pierce looked at his watch.

"Damn!"

"What's the matter, Doctor?"

"Sorry, Jean, I didn't realize the time." He finished writing his notes in a patient's file before snapping the folder closed. "Leave that stuff. Go home. It's late." He waved away her protests.

Jean nodded and hurried with her remaining tasks.

Pierce continued tidying the numerous piles of work on his desk. The work wasn't urgent, but involved nagging, administrative details. Twice a week, not including the weekends, he brought work to his house to complete. Sometimes he could get more done sitting in a comfortable chair with his feet up than in his tight office.

"Have a good night, Doctor."

"See you tomorrow." He finished locking up the office and got into his car.

Once the flow of patients had diminished, his brain had time to reevaluate earlier events with Beth and Haley. His conscience also had the time to make him aware that he was a hypocrite. Earlier he'd cast judgment on Haley when she had made the difficult decision to go back to work instead of staying with Beth. He should have backed her up. He would've alleviated some of her guilt and some of her daughter's anger. Instead he'd remained silent, lining up for his turn to condemn her. He didn't have to get involved, but standing by, doing nothing wasn't in his nature.

With guilt twisting his gut, he took the right on Houston Road toward Haley's, rather than a left toward his house. He dialed her number on his cell phone. She probably wasn't home yet. It didn't matter that she wasn't there. Actually, it gave him more time to put his plan in motion. According to his watch, he had about half an hour to set up all the details.

He wanted to assuage his guilty feelings about the afternoon and make things up to her. There was no way that he could go home and fix himself dinner knowing that Beth was sitting home alone. Beth had told him that Lezlie left at seven.

One more detour proved necessary. A few minutes later, he ended at Laura's condo. "I need your help, sis."

"Good evening to you, too. This is a first. Go on."

"Would you come with me to Mom's house? This is pretty important." Thank goodness she was dressed, so that he wouldn't lose time.

"Why?" She crossed her arms, not budging.

"I'll explain in the car. Oh, and bring some food to make a meal for dinner."

She was almost out the door with him before she pulled away from his hand. "What are you up to? Is this a plan to get back into Sheena's good graces?"

"I'm not thinking about Sheena nor everyone's hang-ups." He was tired of wearing the bad-guy label. Haley and Beth had touched him in a very personal way. He had no regrets, despite the family's strong disapproval.

"Looks like you got your fight back. Well, now you've got my interest. How can I help?"

"I have to take dinner to a girl."

"You know I woke up today thinking that it would be another boring day. But you are constantly surprising me tonight. You've got a girl-friend?"

"She's thirteen."

"Hmm. What about the mother?" She leaned over and pulled his earlobe, a reminder of how she'd nagged him as a little girl.

"I'll fill you in to keep you from harassing me." He briefed her on the day's events. "I know that Beth's mother will be home shortly, but she'll be tired. I didn't want to go over to the house with only Beth there. Not quite appropriate, you know."

"I'd say not. I don't understand why you're getting into the private lives of these people. I thought all you were doing was collecting the check from the property-management company and occasionally fixing an appliance. Listening to you, makes me think that you've taken things to a more personal level. Are these your new bud-dies? I can't wait to call Sheena."

"Touch that phone and you die."

She poked him in the chest. "My big brother is playing big daddy."

"Coming, no or yes?" He waited a second before turning and heading to his car. Maybe he'd buy fast food and simply drop it off with Beth.

"Relax. I'm coming. I've never seen you so worked up over another family. Or is this all about the mother? Haley, is it? Glad to see that we're not the only ones that you've sunk your teeth into." His sister wore a smug smile as she winked at him.

"I swear, I think you've been taking pain-in-the-butt lessons from Sheena."

"You're making me feel sorry for you. It's your lucky day. I baked a large pan of lasagna at the beginning of the week. I have cornbread and a three-bean salad. They're all in containers in the refrigerator. You're welcome to all of it."

"Really?" He hugged his sister. "I take back all my recent insults."

The moment Pierce stood in front of Haley's door poised to knock, he grew a bit nervous. Would she think of his help with Beth as an intrusion or would she thank him for being thoughtful? He'd already called Beth to let her know that he was coming over with his sister.

Once they were inside and introductions were out of the way, Laura took over the logistics, distributing the various tasks. Beth had to set the table. Pierce gathered the ingredients for a garden salad and Laura reheated the food. With only fifteen minutes to spare before Haley arrived, the table was laden with a full-course meal.

Pierce's mother had often scolded him on his pride. If she were still with them, she'd click her tongue and shake her head at his current boastful thoughts. He couldn't help it. Laura and Beth had done a great job with the table, making it look homey and inviting.

"All we can do is wait." He gestured to the living room where they had planned to surprise Haley.

Less than a minute later, they heard the key in the lock. He tried not to stare at the front door.

"Beth, I'm home." Haley dropped her pocketbook and keys on the side table. She looked up and immediately took a step back. "Pierce, what are you doing here?" Her smile was replaced by a worried frown. "Good grief, did something else happen?"

"No. No." Pierce popped out of the chair and went to her side. "It's all right." He wanted to smooth the frown from her forehead. Even if she didn't have a frown, he wanted to touch her face, taste her lips, hold her in his arms.

Beth came up beside them. "Surprise, Mom!"

Haley didn't respond, but she didn't have to. The broad grin on her face said it all. When she'd walked through the door, her shoulders were drooped, her face shadowed with obvious fatigue. Pierce couldn't be more satisfied to see delight brighten her features. Already he was thinking of what more he could do to keep that joy in place.

"Who did all of this?" Haley looked at Beth. "I was driving home wondering what I could scrape together for a meal. My head hurt, my feet ached, my body felt like a truck ran over it." She walked around the table, shaking her head. "How did you prepare all of this?" Haley asked no one in particular. She hugged her daughter. And looking over Beth's head, her eyes didn't leave Pierce's face. She mouthed, "Thank you."

"Haley, meet my sister Laura. She is the savior of the day."

The two women shook hands. He knew

Laura's sharp mind was recording every detail of the interaction between him and Haley and his ease with Beth. Undoubtedly she would pass her findings on to the rest of the Masterson clan. Sheena would be contacting him in time for the upcoming weekend. Her curiosity would be too much to handle. Tonight's happenings would get him access to the family dinner for sure. His ticket to the Sunday fete would be having his brain picked clean.

Haley had walked through the door completely exhausted by the day's events. She grew more tired when she thought about the evening's to-do list. She had promised to watch TV with Beth; she would have to make dinner, and some time during the evening, she would have to lecture Beth about her recent behavior.

Her main thought had been to kick off her pumps and slide out of her panty hose. Whoever had invented control-top stockings must have hated women, she'd thought tiredly. She'd unzipped her skirt, enjoying some freedom, before unlocking her front door.

She'd had to grab her skirt to keep it from falling when she'd realized that she had company.

She was frazzled, but all she could be was grateful for Pierce's kindness to Beth. At least she got the added benefit of seeing him after thinking about him all afternoon. One look at his face and those sculpted lips and she was ready to climb over the chairs to get to him.

Thinking about kissing him caused her to blush. She put a hand to her cheek to see if her skin was as hot as she felt inside. "I'm going to head upstairs before we settle down to eat. I need to get out of these clothes."

"I know what you mean," Laura acknowledged with a chuckle. "I did the same thing as soon as I got home. The hose was the first thing to go."

Haley held on tightly to her skirt and headed to her room. She didn't linger over the clothing selection. Everyone was casual except Pierce, who she suspected had come directly from work.

"Hey, Mom." Beth poked her head through the door.

"Come in, sweetheart."

"Wasn't this an awesome surprise? The doc is a pretty cool guy."

"Yes, he is." Haley fluffed out her hair, which had gone askew after she'd pulled a blouse over her head. "Hey, kiddo, am I forgiven?" Haley turned to look in Beth's face trying to read if she remained angry with her.

"Only if you've forgiven me."

"Nice touch. I'll forgive you, but we still need to talk and you're still on punishment."

"Okay."

"Can you believe it, we've got company. Bet you didn't think that I'd ever say that any time soon?"

"You're right, Mom. And we've got food that's getting cold."

"First one at the table is the queen for a day." Haley ran down the stairs, leaping from the third step to the bottom with a loud whoop. Beth wasn't far behind as they rounded the corner with arms and elbows blocking each other.

Sensing a loss, she bumped Beth with her hip and ran full speed to the table. "Queen for a day!" Haley yelled in triumph. She immediately felt as if she'd interrupted brother and sister, or shocked Pierce and Laura by her juvenile behavior. She shrugged. "It's a mother-daughter thing."

"Didn't say a word." Pierce stepped behind her chair and pulled it out. His hand lingered on her shoulder before he took his seat.

She reached for a glass of water. She might

need a steady serving of ice cubes to get her through the night. "I'm starved."

"Then let's eat." Pierce served each of the ladies at the table a large square of lasagna, before serving himself.

Haley inhaled the bold aroma of tomatoes, garlic and cheese. Her stomach pangs urgently sent her a message to stop inhaling and start eating. "Laura, this is so delicious. I love three-bean salad."

"Thanks. We all helped. You may have noticed the formal setting of the table. Beth wanted to show off her secret talent."

Beth looked mortified at the attention. Haley restrained herself from grabbing her daughter and showering her with kisses. She looked at her plate. "Aren't you eating?"

"Pacing myself. I'm starting with the three-bean salad."

Haley didn't know why Beth always talked about herself as if she were overweight or chubby. She hoped it was a phase. It worried her that her daughter's cheeks were so hollow. She'd have to keep an eye out for signs that Beth had a serious problem with food and dieting.

"I'm loving all of it." Haley helped herself to a

forkful of lasagna. She didn't want to indulge her overactive imagination. "This sauce is to die for."

"Actually Pierce taught me how to make it when we were kids. We used cheaper substitute ingredients and had to spread it a long way."

"And who taught you, Pierce?" Haley wanted to know as much as she could about this thoughtful, handsome man.

"My mother taught me how to make easy recipes. As I got older, I experimented."

"He was an ogre. We had to tell him that it tasted good or he'd have his nose out of joint."

Everyone at the table erupted in laughter. Haley looked at Pierce over the top of her glass. He had a charming manner that would always serve to make him the center of attention. She watched him as he gave Beth his undivided attention, asking pertinent questions, joking with her, lightening her mood. Haley wished that she could get a guarantee that this lightheartedness could last for a long time.

"Haley, I've heard so much about you. I'm glad that we finally met," Laura said. "No need to worry. It's been all good. I've been wondering, do you have any friends in Hampton Mews?"

"No. And since I'm working long hours, I

haven't been able to know my neighbors. But I'm planning a cookout and will invite my friends and brothers."

"Brothers?"

"Two brothers, Stan and Theo. My parents are still around, but I'm not sure whether they will make the drive. I wish that they would attend, since they haven't seen the house at all."

"Here's hoping that they can come." Pierce held up his glass of iced tea and everyone else followed.

Laura stifled a yawn. "I hate to eat and run, but I think that my energy level is taking a nosedive."

"Don't apologize. As soon as I clean up, I'll be hitting the bed." Haley might have felt fatigued when she'd first come home, but seeing Pierce and spending time in his company was like a shot of caffeine to her system.

"We'll help clean up, so that's not a burden." Pierce took charge of the cleanup process. He was adamant that she not do anything.

"Since I'm sitting here doing nothing, I've come up with a plan," Haley said. "Why don't I return the favor? Let me fix brunch for the both of you. This Saturday?"

"That sounds great to me," Pierce said.

"That does sound good," Laura said. "But I'm afraid I've already made plans to go antiquing early Saturday morning," Laura said to Haley. "Hey, how about I take a rain check, you and Pierce enjoy brunch and you let Beth come antique shopping with me?"

"Oh, Mom, please? Say yes."

"Hey, I didn't mean to put your mom on the spot…"

Haley looked at Beth, amazed at the girl's transformation. She seemed to blossom under Laura's attention. Maybe their relationship was so volatile because Beth didn't have enough social interaction with other people.

Having brunch with Pierce on Saturday morning paled in comparison to waking up next to him. Now where had that thought come from, Haley wondered.

"Beth can go," Haley said before she lost her nerve.

Chapter 5

On Saturday, Beth and Laura got an early start on their adventure to West Virginia. Haley offered to make brown-bag lunches, but they wrinkled their noses at the suggestion. They had already planned their day, which included visiting a highly recommended family-owned restaurant in the neighborhood.

After they left, Haley considered sliding back into bed and savoring a few more hours of lazy indulgence. The other option was vacuuming and dusting, washing several loads of laundry and mopping the kitchen floor. With a loud groaning stretch, she scratched her stomach and headed for the stairs. Maybe after she slept for another couple hours, she'd have the energy to complete and generate some excitement for her household chores.

If Beth thought she'd gotten away without tasks, she would be surprised at the list being held by two magnets that had been placed on the refrigerator door. Cleaning the basement and organizing their storage boxes should take a good week. Haley left that burden to Beth. She suspected that her daughter would protest the assignment with lots of logic and teenage angst.

Someone knocked at the door.

"For heaven's sake, go away," she muttered as she stomped back down the stairs. She hoped that it wasn't some kid trying to sell cookies or magazines. *No* wasn't in her vocabulary. Inevitably she'd buy out their inventory or add magazines, like *Horse Breeders,* to her reading list.

She opened the door ready to battle.

"Pierce?" Her pulse did its usual flip-flop, causing that annoying hitch in her breath that made her voice sound whispery.

"Good morning. Got a call from Laura that

they were on the road." Pierce held up several bulging shopping bags in each hand. "You did promise to treat me to brunch, but I decided to do the honors."

His boyish grin disarmed her. She'd forgotten all about her offer. But there he stood with groceries in hand, in a crisp white polo shirt—chiseled forearms revealed—tucked into navy-blue pants. "I like a man bearing breakfast," she told him with a teasing smile.

For the next few hours her taste buds would feast on breakfast, while her eyes would feast on Pierce.

"What's that?" She tilted her chin to the bags on the counter. Some of their contents spilled, revealing a carton of buttermilk, flour and eggs.

"Breakfast. There will be no frozen pancakes for heating up in the toaster oven. And we're not consuming any preserved bacon that sits on a regular, unrefrigerated shelf."

"Have you been looking in my pantry?" She picked up the box of instant oatmeal and restored it to its spot in the cupboard next to the stove.

"Didn't want to risk you not having key ingredients. Plus, I'm always prepared. Cuts down on surprises and delays."

"Then you're missing out on spontaneous fun."

"I'm as spontaneous as the next guy." He took out the potatoes and washed them. "Just not right now."

"Name one thing that you've done that was impulsive." She took a bowl out of the dishwasher and set it on the counter. Then she took the egg carton and a fork. Pierce came over and took the eggs from her.

"Here's an impulsive act for you. Going into a dirty storage shed to look for a nonexistent cat," he said.

"Not exciting, but acceptable."

"Allowing a teenager to draw a mural in my waiting room."

"Dangerous, but not really sexy," she replied.

"Making love to you right after we eat," he murmured.

Haley wished that she had a witness. The lack of sleep had muddled her brains and her hearing. Pierce didn't seem affected by the statement. Meanwhile her body tingled on hyper-mode. She fidgeted with the bags, her clothes, her hair. She bit her lip to keep hysterical giggles from erupting from her mouth.

"That doesn't count as spontaneous." She took

a deep breath. The image of her and Pierce getting their groove on did weird things to her belly and beyond. "Sounds more like an ulterior motive."

"The thought didn't enter my mind until your arm brushed against mine when I took the eggs." He tossed the cleaned potato in a bowl with the others. "But if it doesn't qualify, then I'll have to think of something else."

"No, don't do that. Obviously you're working on being a genuine shoot-from-the-hip sort of man. I don't want to discourage you. Let's take that idea and work with it."

Pierce nodded and continued with his task, taking each potato and chopping them into bite-size pieces. The water had already started to boil. He scooped up the potato pieces and carefully deposited them into the water.

"How long is all this going to take?" She looked up at the kitchen clock hung over the window. "I'm not that hungry. A bowl of Beth's cereal will suffice."

"Sorry, that won't do. I came over to make a wonderful breakfast. No deviations from that plan." He cracked an egg and dropped it into a bowl.

"Feed me? Then ravish me?" She took out a

can of whip cream, broke the seal and sprayed a dollop directly in her mouth. "Guess I'll surrender my turf to you." She motioned with her head. "I'm going to freshen up."

Pierce didn't answer. He was too busy whipping the eggs into a frothy mixture. She surveyed the area. Her quiet kitchen had been transformed into a hub of activity with various sizes of bowls filled with contents for the morning's meal.

Haley turned her face up to the stream of water shooting from the shower head. The cool water refreshed her as her mind entertained steamy thoughts. She laughed into the water flowing over her face. A man was in her kitchen waiting to make love to her. The scenario should be normal, except that her life hadn't been normal since she'd arrived in Hampton Mews.

Two options lay ahead of her. She could dress, eat breakfast and refuse the rest of Pierce's game plan. Or she could eat her breakfast with a high level of anticipation.

Her stomach growled. The aroma of vanilla and cinnamon spiced the air, along with the tasty smell of bacon and eggs. She finished dressing quickly. With a few drops of expensive perfume dabbed on her neck, cleavage, thighs and dimpled indentations over her butt for good measure, she snapped the bottle closed and examined her entire look in the mirror.

She kept the makeup light and fluffed out her damp hair, allowing it to curl in lazy waves to her shoulders. The soft pink halter outfit with fifties-style skirt had a mixture of current in-your-face fashion and nostalgic TV moms fashion. She could spice up the outfit with her white sandals. Instead she wanted to dress for her approval, not to please someone else. She wanted comfort. Most of all, she wanted to maintain her style. Pierce liked control and order. She wanted to break the rules. She headed for the kitchen with bare feet and a toe ring in place.

"Oh, my gosh." Haley's mouth dropped open. The kitchen had been cleaned. Dishes had disappeared into the dishwasher. The countertop had been wiped with a bleach cleanser. Even the dust bunnies in the corners of the kitchen were gone.

Pierce stood behind one chair, which he pulled out, and waited. Her feet were rooted to the spot. She'd never expected anything close to this magnitude. The dining table bore the result of Pierce's handiwork. From one end of the table, placed in a line down the middle, she saw French toast, scrambled eggs, Polish sausages, fried breakfast potatoes, sliced fruit and orange juice that she confidently surmised had to be freshly squeezed.

"I need you to take a seat. I have to check the muffins."

Haley obeyed, thanking him as she pulled her seat to the table. Then he retrieved a tray of blueberry muffins that smelled heavenly. Her stomach growled again in protest.

"How did you do all of this?" She'd only been upstairs for twenty minutes.

"I learned to work fast when it came to my brother and sisters." Pierce placed the muffins on a plate and brought them to the table.

"This is such a wonderful treat." Haley took her plate and helped herself to two thick wedge slices of French toast. "You've even sprinkled it with powdered sugar. And chocolate-dipped strawberries? Most men would bring flowers, maybe a bottle of wine, and then make their move."

"I'm not most men. I care about you." He proffered the plate of strawberries. "You might want to eat the strawberries first before the chocolate makes a mess."

"Is this the real you, Pierce Masterson? You're a mother-in-law's dream. Can't believe that you escaped their wily plans on behalf of all daughters-at-large?" She finished off a strawberry, enjoying the mix of the chocolate and fruity sweetness.

"Have no reason to be any other way. Makes life simpler."

"Is that why you've stayed here instead of moving to a busy city?"

"In the beginning, I'd planned to go off and be a doctor in New York. After my mother died, the family needed me. I made the decision to remain. I have no regrets." He ate a forkful of eggs. His gaze steady on her face.

"I care about you, too. You're always thinking about the other person. I find that refreshing and attractive."

"Do you find me an awesome cook?"

"I think that I'll call you Master Chef." She took the last remaining piece of French toast and swirled it in the maple syrup. "I suppose you feel right at home in this kitchen?"

"Standing at the stove did bring back memories. Yet, it's different. The chaotic atmosphere wasn't there." He pointed toward the living room. "Sometimes my mother would come home from her job on the midnight shift. She'd sit in the large winged-back chair and kick off her shoes. I'd make breakfast and she'd talk about her evening. Most times she'd fall asleep before I'd finished cooking. Sheena would cover her with a blanket. I'd keep a plate in the oven." He took a deep breath. Haley could see him try to shake off the memories and the emotions they evoked.

This house with its three levels, lots of windows and large backyard had grown on her. When she'd moved in, the house had been safe harbor out of a depressive life. Over the months, after she had painted, decorated and furnished her home, the old house had settled into her heart. It had character and didn't have that mass-market assembly feel that the new housing tract that was being built on the other side of the city did.

"You had a lot of responsibility for a young boy." She poured a second cup of coffee, adding a dollop of milk and a spoonful of sugar.

"I'll take a cup, too." Pierce slid his mug to Haley. "As much as it hurt, and I thought that I would never recover from what I perceived as my father's betrayal, my situation wasn't unique." He sipped his black coffee. "While we all moped around being angry and having our own pity parties, I knew we couldn't make it if we didn't suck it up and pull together. I took on the role of drill sergeant."

"Jeez, I guess that didn't earn you the Favorite Big Brother Award." Pierce had the height and demeanor to look strict. "Did your sisters ever get to date?"

"Oh, don't start that line of questioning. Thank goodness they aren't here to jump on the bandwagon. In my defense, I did it out of love." He drained his mug.

Haley admired his neck as his Adam's apple bobbed. Was there any part of this man that she didn't find attractive? She'd no doubt that he always sought to take the lead, but with all the unexpected sweet things that he'd done for her, she believed that he had a deep sensitive nature.

She reached across the table and took his hand, bringing it to her cheek. His finger stroked her skin with a tenderness that melted any remaining reservations that threatened her courage. She kissed each of his fingers and experienced a foolish desire to kiss every inch of his body.

"You positively sweet, hunky man, do you do anything for purely selfish reasons? You're killing my stereotypical beliefs." Haley touched her chest and smiled in gratitude. "You've even helped Beth and me out of a difficult situation." She kissed the top of his hand. "Thank you for that. But I've yet to hear you say that you want to do something for yourself." She squeezed his hand, hoping that he truly understood what an impact he'd made in her life. "You must have dreams, Pierce. Share with me…please?"

Pierce lowered his gaze from her face. He didn't need to say anything for her to sense that she'd made him feel uncomfortable. A dark frown covered his features. She was tempted to smooth away the three rows of deep grooves that marred his handsome forehead with a kiss.

He pulled back in his chair. "No offense, but I think that I'll keep my dreams right here," he said as he tapped his temple. "Back to your original question, though, I am doing something for myself. I'm laying the groundwork to have an after-breakfast lovefest with you."

And if Haley passed away this minute, she knew she'd be laid out with a smile on her face.

"I have to clear away the dishes and the food. Later we can have seconds and eat in the backyard."

"Your fastidiousness isn't necessary, you know." Haley pushed away her plate hoping Pierce would take the hint. She licked her lips, tasting the sweet residue of the maple syrup and sat back in what she hoped was a seductive pose.

Pierce shook his head, granting her a toothy grin. He began clearing the dishes, moving methodically back and forth between the dining room and kitchen.

Frustrated that she had to wait, she played with her fork, stirring it in a small pool of syrup. She licked her fork like a lollipop, hoping that Pierce would be moved by her flirtation. In a few minutes, she'd let him taste the sweetness with a lip-locking, toe-curling kiss. Not that she suffered from a massive ego of her abilities. Quite the opposite, her attraction to Pierce opened the door to her lively imagination.

Instead of voicing her frustration, she lent a hand with finding storage containers for the leftovers. Haley glanced at him as he walked past her. She enjoyed the whiff of his aftershave, crisp and spicy.

"I'm beginning to think that you don't have human blood flowing through those veins." He'd given her a peek into his sensual treasure chest, and now he sat atop its closed lid like a genie for no other reason than to send her into agony with the expectation.

"You'll thank me later for not leaving the kitchen a mess," he said.

"I'm turned on by a neat freak," she muttered. Her yearning wasn't all physical lust. He did touch her heart. Pierce had a smooth sophistication that added sexy to his demeanor.

In full pout, she stacked the plates, piled on the silverware and grabbed the cups by their handles before heading to the dishwasher. If Beth had set the dishes in the washer in the same haphazard fashion that she used, she'd have made her daughter redo them.

She wiped down the excess water off the counter, hung the dishcloth on the edge of the sink and waited for Pierce to stop polishing the table.

Wasn't he as hot and decidedly bothered as she? Shouldn't he be flustered? Shouldn't he want to rip off her clothes, right here, right now?

"All done." His voice held such a pride for the good job he'd done in cleaning up the kitchen and dining area.

She walked right up to his face and jabbed her

finger into his chest. "That's what you think. I'm not all done. I haven't begun. I hope that you'll take your time and be as conscientious with me as you were with that table." She planted her hand on the table, leaving her handprint.

Pierce lifted her hand and replaced it at her side. Then he took the cloth and erased the smudge back to its gleam. "I'm known as a man who pays attention to detail."

"Let's see if I can add my recommendation to your testimonials. I'm heading upstairs. I'd hate for this to be a solo venture, but perhaps there's a patient who will get your undivided attention." She walked past him, deliberately adding a sway to her hips with her best come-hither look.

Pierce accepted Haley's unspoken invitation. His hand closed around her slender wrist. She looked up at him, startled, with her mouth slightly parted. Contact with her skin short-circuited his system. If she only knew how touching her sent an electric shock through his body.

He pulled her against him. All the faked calmness he'd displayed had expired and he couldn't hold out any longer. Her hypnotic gaze stroked his heart like a siren's harp.

During breakfast, he wanted to pull his chair

next to hers. The casual passing brush of their arms stoked his addiction for more than her physical beauty. He wanted the inner core that defined her true essence. He blinked, holding his eyes closed for a few seconds. Never had he experienced such powerful emotions. It felt as if his heart was guiding instead of his head.

"Kiss me before my head explodes," she said.

He responded to Haley's demand without hesitation. His mouth covered hers, greedily enjoying the sticky sweetness of maple. Her soft lips spoke a language that he quickly learned and mastered.

His body, on the other hand, stirred with a hunger that couldn't be satisfied with a kiss. Although he drowned in her embrace and the sweetness of her mouth, he wanted more. He drew away from her lips until he could see her eyes.

They had darkened ever so slightly. Her arousal matched his in intensity. He felt sure that she could feel the physical change in him as their bodies were pressed so closely together.

"What's the matter?" she asked in a sultry, thick voice.

"I want you to know that I don't do this with just anyone. I'm not a player. I'm respectful of women. I can't help how strong my feelings are for you. I don't want you to be afraid that I'm going to take advantage of you. I know what a rough time you've had. I'm here for you."

"I appreciate that, Pierce," she said and ran her hand down his stomach. He twitched as he felt her fingers go past his waist and slide over the front of his pants. Her hand settled over his arousal, which responded immediately to her manipulation. "I'd say you're as ready as you're going to be. Shall we stop dawdling?"

Pierce took her hands and pinned her against a wall. "You can't touch like that and expect me to act like a gentleman."

She took no mercy on him, arching her body. The deep V-cut of the halter top gaped and the exposed swell of her breasts teased him. She wrapped a leg around his and slid her hips against him.

"So you think you're ready?" Pierce played with her earlobe, enjoying her moans. He kissed her neck where her pulse visibly beat, resting his lips against her skin as the moans vibrated through her throat.

He lifted her, cradling her against his chest. He didn't want to remove his hands from her body. She wrapped her arms around his neck to stay in place. Her perfume did its part to heighten the reaction of all his senses.

"You think Laura knew that you would seduce me?"

"I figured you had coerced her to do your bidding." Haley kissed his chin.

"No more kissing until we get upstairs. Otherwise, I may drop you." He headed for the stairs. There was no need for her to give him direction. He had grown up in this house.

Haley pointed the way to what was once his mother's room.

He pushed open the door with his foot and glanced around. He was glad to see that the room had changed from the sickly yellow to a creamy blue. The furniture layout, however, copied what he recollected. Haley's vanity sat on the left. The chest of drawers was behind him, supporting the television. There was a small desk and a chair in the right corner of the room. Flesh-tone panty hose hung over the back of the chair.

"Here you are, safe and sound." He walked toward the bed and gently laid her in its middle on a royal-blue comforter.

She pushed herself back toward the matching pillows. He watched her pull the skirt down around her exposed legs. She grinned. Her hazel eyes twinkled full of mischief.

"You are so darn beautiful."

"And you are so darn handsome."

He unbuttoned his shirt.

"No, let me. I want to undress you. You took care of me this morning. I want to take care of you during our time together."

"Only if I get my turn."

"It's a deal." Her hands slid up his chest to his shoulders, sliding the shirt off his back. She planted kisses around his chest, branding him with her mark. "Now for the pants."

"I can't wait," he growled. He grabbed her teasing fingers, sure that his eyes had crossed at least once while she'd traced figure-eights around his belly button.

"I want to memorize your muscle definition." She ran her fingers down his chest; her thumb rubbed against his nipple. His stomach muscles tightened. She unzipped his pants and pushed them down his hips. As if her handling of him weren't enough, she then wrapped her legs around his hips and squirmed in direct contact with his erection. Talking was impossible. He groaned. Or maybe he cried *uncle*.

Pierce had to take a couple deep breaths to fortify his control. She continued to pepper his neck and torso with kisses. In between the kisses, she inflicted agony with flicks of her tongue.

He flipped her so that she now straddled him. Her tousled hair fell forward, partially shielding her face. He smoothed each side back. There was simple pleasure in admiring her face. Her hair peaked in the middle of her forehead and framed the sides of her face, accentuating her narrow chin.

He unfastened her halter and allowed the top to fall. Her breasts lay bare. Their full size, gently sloped, would be an artist's dream. He touched the firm mounds, drawn to their sensitive dark brown peaks.

Haley took his hand, guiding his fingers around her breast. He massaged them, blowing on the peaks to further tease her. Haley didn't back down from the attention. Instead she rocked her hips over him with sensual reciprocation.

He pulled her down and gently covered her nipple with his mouth, coaxing the nub to a taut peak. Her increased moans and shuddering sighs let him know that he pleasured her well. His tongue slowly stroked and teased. His hands slid down to her hips, loving the fleshy cushion of her backside. The lacy panties provided a thin barrier to their ultimate pleasure.

"I want you, but I've got to take care of business first." He eased her over to the side of the bed. He rolled away before swinging his legs to sit on the edge. He grabbed his pants lying on the floor and dug into his pocket for his wallet.

Haley knelt behind him and rested her breasts against his head. Happiness had eluded her for several years. When she'd worked up enough courage to divorce Vernon, happiness had been one of the emotions that she'd figured she'd never experience again. The thought of sharing any part of her life with another man had been buried along with childhood fears and Vernon's nasty criticisms.

She saw the condom wrapper in Pierce's hand. Her pulse did a flip-flop. They were taking the next step together.

"Pierce, I don't want you to think that I want you for more than you're willing to give."

"I understand," he said. "We will be two lonely souls enjoying what the moment brings. No pressure," he said as he looked up at her.

He tore open the small square packet. He

looked toward the morning light that slanted through the open bedroom door. They were both too preoccupied to bother closing it.

He thought about when he would come to his mother's door and hear her weeping after his father had left. His mother's last contact with his father had been a note.

Haley wasn't sure what happened. Pierce stared at the bedroom door. She paused, wondering if he'd heard something. Only his profile was visible. From her vantage point, she could tell that he was thinking. She hesitated before touching his shoulder. He jumped.

"Hey, I think I lost you there for a few seconds."

"Sorry. It's the house. This room." He clutched his pants to his waist.

Haley looked around the room. It was clean, repainted. She thought of it as cozy. "You don't like the room?"

He turned and kissed her hard on the mouth. There was sadness in the act, almost a desperate appeal to her. "It's not the room. I can't help thinking about my mother, which makes me think of my father." He shook his head. "Sorry."

Haley didn't know what to say, except to share

a personal part of herself with him. She pressed her breasts against his back and tried to soothe away the tension from him. "Why don't we go to another room? Perhaps the one on the left— I'm using it as a den."

"Gross, that's Sheena and Laura's room."

"Can't use the one across the hall, that's Beth's." *This magical moment can't be slipping away,* Haley thought. It wasn't fair. Not that she'd planned their lovemaking as part of the morning schedule. But once Pierce had put it out in the open, she'd realized how badly she did want to rub naked bodies with him and reach great climactic pleasure together. "The basement?" she asked weakly, knowing that she didn't care for bedding down with dust and spiders.

The front door closed.

"Mom, we're back!"

Haley kicked Pierce off the bed. "Get in the bathroom." She threw his shirt at him. She'd apologize later. At least he looked as mortified as she did. She hurriedly fastened the top of her halter and pulled on her skirt.

"Laura wasn't feeling well, so we came back. She went on home. I think she was going to throw up," Beth yelled from downstairs.

Haley stood in front of the mirror, fixing her hair. She leaned closer for any signs that she'd been rolling around with a man on her new comforter. As long as Beth didn't come near the stairs, she might be able to distract her so that Pierce could get out of her bathroom.

"Hey, Mom, isn't that doc's car outside?"

"Yes, sweetie. He's fixing the closet door in the guest room."

"Oh, maybe he can fix my window." Beth's voice drew closer.

Haley tiptoed to her bathroom door. "Beth's coming. Hurry up."

"One second," he said, his voice sounding strained. The door opened. He walked out and edged his way against the wall into the guest room.

Beth walked past Haley. At least, she didn't look suspicious. Haley followed her into the guest bedroom. Pierce stood near the bookcase, examining a desk lamp with exaggerated contemplation.

"Hey, Doc."

"Hey, Beth. What's up?"

"Nothing much." Beth stepped closer to him, then stopped. She looked down at his feet. "By the way, where are your shoes?"

Chapter 6

"Mom, Doc said that I could go to his office today and paint."

"It's Sunday, Beth. He couldn't possibly have said that."

"Call him, then."

Haley put down the report that she was reviewing. She had to finish writing her response, which was due the next morning. Beth wasn't letting her concentrate long enough to work.

"Here. Doc is on the line." Beth held out the phone to her.

"Pierce, did you want Beth at the office on Sundays?" She glared at Beth. She hadn't thought that the child would call him.

"Only if someone was in the office, which is rare. Why? Does Beth want to go in?"

"Yes, but it's not going to happen today. I have a lot of work."

"Mom," Beth snarled. "I don't need you to babysit me."

"You can work in my office. I do have some things that I can do there, also," Pierce offered.

Haley knew better than to think that she would be able to work with Pierce in the same office. She would never look at him the same way again. Nothing he wore would erase the enticing image of his almost-naked body, lean and buffed.

"Fine, I'll meet you there." What should have been a lazy afternoon in ratty pants and a big T-shirt had changed to slacks and a blouse.

"Thank you so much, Mom. You're the greatest."

"Yeah, I'm the greatest pushover. Eat your lunch and then we'll go."

Beth sat at the table and nibbled at her lunch of carrots and celery. Haley debated whether to make a fuss about the skimpy, unbalanced meal.

They'd had a few days of relative calm without the emotional swings that she'd come to expect from Beth. At least she was eating.

Haley gathered her work and packed it in her briefcase. She supposed that this was the new version of quality time. They used to sit, huddled together, on the couch in their family room watching a movie, reading a book or playing board games. Now she was lucky to spend a few moments in the same room with her daughter.

The day was overcast. Beth was quiet as they drove to Pierce's office. Haley hoped the rain would hold off until they returned home. She peered up at the thick, gray clouds. Any blue sky that managed to peek through would be short-lived. Haley turned on the radio for any information on the day's weather and to add a bit of background noise to the somber drive. Now that Beth had gotten her way, she was silent, staring out of the window.

"How's school? Seems like things are settling down." At least no other business owner had placed an emergency call about her daughter's latest passion, Haley thought.

"Fine, I guess."

"I think that it's more than fine. You don't

complain about the homework. You've gone to the movies a couple times with your friends. You haven't talked about your friends at the old neighborhood." Beth looked at her as if she'd grown two heads.

"Mom, please. I don't fit in. Sure I get invited. But most places you won't let me go. I have a babysitter as if I'm a little kid. I'm the only one of my friends with day care. It only takes one time when I'm hanging out with people to know that we're not on the same wavelength."

"It's been less than six months. Don't you think that you're being hard on yourself? If I recall, I do allow you to go out. Now you're mad at me because I need to know the details of where you'll be? That's called good parenting." Haley kept her voice even, although her defenses had shot up.

"I'm letting you know that you're being overprotective. When your life doesn't go as planned, you'll probably uproot me and move from here, too. I know the doc is interested in you. One day he might not be anymore. Then, once again, I'll be the one dragging around behind you."

"Where is this coming from? Two minutes ago, you were begging me to do something for you. Now you're overstepping your bounds and talking to me with no respect." Haley pulled over and parked in a gas-station lot. "I'm not going to demand an apology. But let's get something straight." Haley spoke slowly, enunciating each word. She had to calm down. This was her thirteen-year-old daughter. Opening the car door and telling her to get out was not an option, however tempting.

"I am overprotective, as you call it, because there are dangers out here. I can't shield you from everything, but I can take the upper hand and keep tabs on your whereabouts. As your mother, I do have a say in where and when you should go. I don't always agree with the liberties that your friends have, but I'm not their parent. I'm yours. When you make poor judgments like you did with Pierce's property, I have no choice but to come down hard on you. You've got to earn my trust again." She took a deep breath, searching Beth's face for a break in her petulant frown. "And I thought that you didn't have a problem with me seeing Pierce. I'm very considerate of not mixing our times together too much. I don't know where that will go, but I'm enjoying his company now." Haley took a moment to pull herself together. Her hands shook slightly. She had to take a couple deep breaths to focus on what she was doing. Should she turn the car around and head home?

Her daughter's accusation that she'd run and would always run sliced through her like an annoying paper cut. To the naked eye, it seemed like a small remark buried among other unsavory remarks. But the perception stung, its venom resonating through her entire system. She'd hoped that time would heal whatever ailed them, individually and as a family unit. It appeared that time had run out and now she'd have to step up and do something.

Haley turned the key in the ignition. She turned up the music and resumed driving toward Pierce's office. She looked with a critical eye at the older homes that lined the street. They all had the white picket fences, U.S. flags waving from the porches, windows and even doors open. People walked their dogs. Some were in-line skating. Kids played with each other as they ran around in the public playground. She had yearned for this type of nostalgia in her wholesome community and she thought she had found it here.

"This is home. I'm sorry that you're missing out while you're in your adjustment period. But one day when you're not too angry with me, look at everything and the people around you. You'll see that you can make home wherever you are." Haley didn't know how or why they could go from a decent conversation, sharing laughs, to contempt. Beth had a knack for delivering her words with matter-of-fact indifference, but lately her reaction dripped with attitude that seemed hateful.

"As you say, this is my home whether I like it or not, right?" Beth glared at her.

"Sometimes a parent has to do what is right for the child."

"Thought I had two parents."

Haley felt her anger rise. "I'm not trying to erase your father. When I say that I want a fresh start, it does not mean that I'm erasing our past as a family. But you've got to look forward to new, exciting things, situations, even friends that you will meet here. This small city has everything that we need without the hassles of a big-city life. Give it a chance, give me a chance. I know that you will make friends, good ones." Haley didn't miss Beth's rolling of her eyes.

"Dad said that if I wanted to I could stay with him to see if I liked it." Beth looked down in her lap. Each fingernail had a different color. She wore several rubber bands of similar colors around her wrist.

"When did you talk to him?" Haley kept her expression neutral. She congratulated herself that she could stop for the red traffic light and put on her signal to turn while discussing Vernon.

Once she had settled in, she'd let Vernon's lawyer know where they were and how she could be reached.

"Dad called this morning on my cell phone. He was on travel for his job."

"Cell phone?" She didn't recall buying a cell phone.

"Daddy sent it to me in the mail. Don't worry, you don't have to pay for it."

Haley pulled into the parking lot. She didn't see any sign of Pierce. Only one car was in the lot and it was at the far end of the property. They must have beat him here, which worked out fine for this conversation.

"Is having us live so far from our first home making it expensive for Dad to keep in touch with me?"

"I don't know your father's finances. When it's time for you to visit, I will get you there."

"I miss him."

"I know it must be hard," Haley answered with care. She wasn't going to sink to the lowest level to talk about Vernon's shortcomings. So far, she'd tried to keep their lives at status quo. Maybe Beth needed to see the hard realities of being a single parent a few times to make her more appreciative.

"You don't know how hard it is. Grandmom and Granddad are still married. So how could you know? Uncle Theo and Stan aren't married," Beth said.

"When I had you, I forgot about the unhappy times in my marriage because you were my special gift. But I couldn't overcome the difficulties singlehandedly." She raised Beth's chin. They had similar eye coloring, along with other physical features. "Beth, I want you to know that I'm doing the best I can to make a better life for you and me. I don't mind talking to you, but let's do just that—talk, not fight." She kissed her daughter's cheek and felt the dampness of her tears. "Do you want to go home? I'll make the excuse to Pierce."

Beth didn't look up from her lap. Her hands were meekly clasped. "I promised Doc that I'd finish by this week. Plus he could have been really mean about messing up his fence." Beth wiped her face. Haley dug in her pocketbook and handed Beth a tissue.

"How much of the mural do you have left?"

"Doc hired a painter to help me finish it."

"Talk about being a pushover. I hope you told him thank you." Haley knew that Pierce hadn't done it to get on Beth's good side. He had a kind heart and did what he was impelled to do. Still, she was shocked by his generosity.

"I thanked him. I really like Doc. I didn't want to…" Beth said.

"Thank you for being honest. I like him, too."

Just then Pierce pulled into the space next to them. He offered them a wide grin and waved. His playful attitude raised both their spirits as they got out of the car and exchanged friendly greetings.

"Look, Beth, I'll talk to your father and see what we can work out. I don't want you to linger over this stuff. Enjoy school, make friends, have fun," Haley said softly before pulling her daughter into a hug.

"You're so corny, Mom. I love you."

"Yeah, well, eat something for heaven's sake. All I feel is bones."

Haley walked hand in hand with Beth on one side and Pierce on the other. If she measured today's conversation as a milestone, she wasn't sure how much ground she'd covered, but at this moment, they all appeared to be happy.

Beth got underway with her wall. A large canvas drop cloth protected the carpet and furniture. An opaque plastic sheet hung from scaffolding shielded the wall from view. Haley tried to get a preview, but Beth forbade her. She'd have to wait until the unveiling.

Haley had to admit she felt proud that her daughter had a passion that brought her fulfillment. If painting was what it took to keep a smile on Beth's face, Haley would raid the craft stores for paints, brushes and anything else that the salesperson wanted to sell her.

Feeling a little more settled, she now could delve into her work. She followed Pierce to the offices in the back of the building. He showed her an empty office next to his, equipped with a desk and credenza.

"It's awfully quiet back here." Haley set down her laptop. The waiting room seemed far away.

"Believe me, it's buzzing around here during business hours. Sometimes I come back here for a little peace and quiet." He leaned casually against the door frame.

"You got a haircut. Looks good," Haley complimented, admiring his tapered sides, clean and
sharp. The last time she'd seen or talked to Pierce
was last week when he'd fielded Beth's question
about his feet. The grand finale of their lovefest
still brought a chuckle to her lips.

"Coffee? I could start the machine," he offered.

"Thanks, but I'll pass. How about sodas? Iced
tea, maybe?"

"Sure," he said. He walked away. Then she
heard his footsteps return and he popped his head
in the doorway. "You okay? Not that I expect you
to show the same laugh-out loud hilarity at my
psychological bedroom hang-ups. But you looked
pensive a few minutes ago. Beth barely looked at
me when she came in. Want to talk?"

Haley didn't talk about Vernon with Pierce.
She wasn't ready to do that. She shook her head.
"Please understand…."

"No problem. As usual I want to jump right in
to fix the problem. After dealing with my sisters,
you'd think I'd learn." He laughed.

"You are so fantastic that I could hug you." She
raised her hand to stop his advance. "Not
now…Beth." With her daughter's obvious inse-
curity and confusion about her father, and Haley's

relationship with Pierce, the last thing Beth needed was to catch Haley and Pierce smooching. Pierce nodded. He was in a profession where it was important to keep emotional distance and keep his feelings private. She couldn't tell if he was offended.

"I'll get your drink." In less than a minute, he returned with the soda. "You can get access to the Internet using dial-up. I'm next door if you need me."

Pierce's departure made her feel lonely in the small, bare office. Being able to sit and work without interruptions was good, but she couldn't concentrate knowing that Pierce was next door.

Her cursor blinked on the screen waiting for her input. Either she forced her mind to crank out the information that her boss needed, or she'd be up all night struggling to meet her deadline. She'd have to log on to the Internet to gain access to her company's database. Critical information for one section resided in the common folder on the company's network.

Haley worked steadily, gulping down her iced tea and chewing a tasteless, sugar-free gum. Beth popped in her head for vending-machine money. Haley didn't look up, waving her in the direction of her pocketbook. Even Pierce tried to get her attention about another soft drink. She nodded, but didn't allow her fingers to slow down. She had the conclusion to write and then she could send this report to her boss, Strayer, and a few other department heads.

Ever since she had landed Thadeus Bedford as a client, Strayer had sung her praises. She was becoming his go-to person. At first, the honor had only come when another employee was out or unavailable. But her response time and follow-up had raised her above a few peers. Haley enjoyed someone respecting her talent and worth. Though she had had to skip a few family moments because of work, it had been worth it. She would make up the time with Beth, Haley promised. And being appreciated at work gave Haley's self-confidence a much needed boost.

An e-mail notice popped onto her screen. Haley didn't recognize the sender. The subject line stated: Thinking of You. Intrigued, but leery that the mail was an intro to an X-rated site, Haley clicked open the note.

Didn't want anything. Simply making sure that you're thinking about me. I can't stop thinking of you. Looking forward to connecting the dots.

Love to also think about you. Can't wait for you to connect the dots. Where oh where will that be?

Haley remembered Pierce taking his finger and tracing the moles around her body. He had counted three and had been on the hunt for more. She crossed her legs, recalling that one was on her inner thigh, another on her left breast and another on her neck near her jaw. Pierce had sucked each spot, claiming he wanted to leave his own beauty mark.

Part 2—a continuation was part of my plan, all along. My place. Next Friday. We'll start at the driving range. Eat dinner at the country club. Settle in for the night at my place.
P.S. Laura said okay to look after Beth. They're going to have a slumber party.

Can't wait. :-)

Haley leaned back in the chair, feeling wicked at the rush of excitement and giddy anticipation for the weekend.

The morning started off as any other morning. Haley added a light cover of foundation and would finish up with her favorite reddish-brown lip color. Since she had completed the reports and e-mailed back to her job, her mind was relaxed.

Beth had already left for school. She hadn't yelled goodbye as she'd headed out the door, but Haley had heard the front door close. Haley had looked out the window in Beth's room to catch a glimpse of her daughter turning the corner at the end of the street.

When Haley moved away from the window, she glanced around the room. She couldn't get on Beth's case about having a messy room. Her daughter had everything in its place. The bed was neatly made. Beth had even dusted the shelves. Haley made a mental note to compliment Beth for keeping her room shipshape.

However, Beth had left the radio on. The volume had been turned down, but the DJ's voice still filled the room. Haley turned up the radio, listening to the exchange between the DJ and his partner. The jokes were off-color, a sign of the times, and then a hip-hop song blasted the air. Another time, she may have changed stations to a mellow music program, but today she could bear the floor-shaking, head-throbbing beat, especially since she returned to her bedroom. The distance helped soften the bass.

In front of the bathroom mirror, her head bopped and her feet tapped. She added a light coating of eye shadow. Why not? Ever since Pierce had invited her on a date for Friday, she'd been counting down the days.

She set down her makeup and paused, listening. Her phone was definitely ringing. Haley picked up the phone, sensing that this couldn't be good. She tried to fasten her earring while she pressed the phone to her other ear. "Yes," she answered, not holding back her impatience.

"This is the vice principal, Fiona Wilkes, at Hampton Mews Middle School. I'd like to speak to Beth Sanders's parent."

"This is Haley Sanders, her mother." Haley placed a weary hand across her brow. "What's the matter with Beth?" she prompted.

"We ran the morning attendance report and she is listed as absent. We make routine, random calls to verify the absences."

"Beth is not here. Do you have her listed for any other absences?"

"No, Ms. Sanders."

"I'll be in touch with the school once I learn her whereabouts." Haley finished the phone call, barely able to talk or listen to anything further the vice principal had to say.

She dropped her pocketbook onto a side table, next to the keys. She punched in the numbers to her work. Briefly she told her assistant that she would be late. Then she placed another call.

"Laura, glad I caught you before you left for work. Have you seen Beth? Her school called because she didn't show up today."

"No, the last time I saw her was the day we went to West Virginia."

"Did she say anything, you know, about any issues going on here? I'm not much of a confidante these days."

"She didn't say too much. Do you need me to come over? I don't have a meeting until eleven."

"No, I'll handle this. But I may be calling you later." She hung up the phone at a loss as to where to begin her search.

She wondered if Beth was trying to make her

way back to Vernon. Her stomach pitched at the thought of Beth standing on the side of a highway thumbing a ride.

She dialed her ex-husband. The phone rang until it went to voice mail. "Vernon, it's about Beth. I need you to call me. It's important." As much as it pained her to let him know that Beth was missing, she needed his help.

She looked down at the phone wishing that she could call Pierce. He could provide her with the strength and support she needed. But this was a family matter. Although he had come through for her, she didn't want to impose on him.

Beth walked through the back door. Her eyes were red and puffy. She dropped her backpack, but Haley stopped her with a hand on Beth's arm as the girl tried to hurry past her. Her heart sank as Beth wormed her arm away from her hand.

"I'm glad that you're safe. But what's going on with you? I can't believe that you're acting so irresponsibly."

"I wasn't feeling well so I came home."

"School started over an hour ago. Where were you?"

"I walked around. Look, I'm not feeling well."

"Don't you walk away from me." Haley used

an icy tone to deliver the command. "You talk to me before I make you talk."

Beth looked up at her and sniffed loudly. "*It* happened."

"I'm supposed to know what *it* means?" Haley frowned. What the heck was *it?* Did they talk about *it?* She'd need some help to figure out what *it* was.

"My first time, Mom."

Haley's eyes opened wide. She could actually feel them ready to pop out of her head. She placed her hand tentatively on Beth's shoulders and guided her up the stairs. Puberty's debut had its own schedule. She'd be lucky if she made it into work before noon. Life sure didn't let up. Dealing with the situation meant more than showing Beth what to do.

At one o'clock, Haley pushed opened the glass door to her job. She'd walked past most of her peers on the way to lunch. People were huddled in their lunch groups fully immersed in their conversations. No one paid her any attention. She took the elevator up to her floor. First she'd check in with Strayer to make sure that he didn't have a problem with her calling in.

She went to his office and peeked in. His chair was pushed in, computer screen dark. Maybe he hadn't come in today. But Vera had said that she would give him her message. Thank heavens, she'd have a few more minutes to settle in before he summoned her to his office.

There was no one in sight to give her a fore-warning about Strayer's mood. His assistant was apparently taking advantage of his absence to extend her lunch hour. Her desk looked cleaned with chair pushed in. Her crocheted wrap was gone. She'd probably headed out for lunch with the gang.

If Strayer was in a good mood, he'd laugh and joke with her. Maybe he'd even tell her that she was a valued employee. If she was unlucky, he would be in a bad mood. Then he'd not only lecture her, but dump the next few lousy assign-ments on her desk. She'd seen this mood-swing dynamic play out between her boss and other co-workers in the past.

Haley headed back to her office. She checked her messages. She had several e-mails. She scrolled through the highlighted list looking for any messages from her boss. Seeing none, she clicked on the message about an all-staff meeting.

She'd missed it. Where was Vera when she needed information? Her assistant kept her in the loop for the office gossip and politics.

Maybe she should look at the other e-mails to get a clue of the morning's event.

"Glad to see that you could make it to work, Haley."

"Mr. Jackson, you startled me. Yes, I got here as soon as I could." This could not be a good sign that her boss's boss stood in her doorway. He didn't look as if he was about to move on after throwing a casual greeting her way.

"Let me close the door. I want to discuss some serious matters with you."

The fact that he hadn't said this with a smile put her on full alert. Her body broke out into an instant sweat. She watched him take a seat opposite hers.

"Mr. Strayer is no longer with the company." He pinned her with a stare.

She didn't know how to react. Was he delivering the news to see where her loyalties lay? For the time being, she would keep silent.

"Several members of the staff were let go this morning. The company is undergoing a reorganization to increase efficiencies. This department had the greatest restructuring to be done."

Haley couldn't speak even if she wanted to. Her body now shook as if an air-conditioning unit were on full blast. All she could do was stare at Jackson's mouth and hope that her hearing still worked to recognize her name when he said that she no longer worked there.

"I know that you've only been with us a short while, but the reports that Strayer provided of your performance impressed the senior staff. As a result we are giving you Strayer's job. I know that you will need additional training. Not to worry, you'll get whatever you need. I'm going to take you under my wing and show you the ropes. Congratulations. Let me know when you'll have your first meeting with your staff." Jackson stood and adjusted his jacket before thrusting his hand out to her. Haley accepted the power handshake. She smiled, but wasn't sure if she only bared her teeth or actually smiled.

After Jackson left her office, Haley looked back at the list of emails. She clicked on them to see how many of them were offers of congratulation. She couldn't help the cowardly thought that at least she hadn't seen the humiliating departure of her boss. She wouldn't have survived here without him. Her promotion had come at too high of a cost. She didn't feel victorious at the moment.

Chapter 7

"Haley, Mr. Jackson wants to see you immediately."

"Thanks, Vera." Haley stared at the framed print on her wall as her assistant's voice relayed the message over the speakerphone. When *didn't* Jackson need to see her immediately, urgently, right now, as soon as possible? His office, located at the other end of the floor, had the prime view of the local city park and man-made lake.

With the constant walking between Jackson's office and her current office for quick meetings,

she figured that she'd discovered her latest
weight-loss plan. No one had mentioned that she
move into Strayer's office. As she adjusted to the
nuances that came with the promotion, she tried
not to appear as if she didn't want this responsibility.

By Wednesday, her body continued its accli-
mation to the long hours and added responsibility.
Only the rare lunch hour out of the building
afforded her the sun's warmth on her skin. She left
home a half hour earlier and was not home before
dark. Her eating had turned erratic with only two
main meals and lots of diet cola. She rarely got
to sleep before midnight. Her availability for
Friday's date night with Pierce looked bleak.

"Mr. Jackson, you called." Haley used her
perky tone and bit back using the term *summoned*.

"Good, I'm glad I caught you before you got
down to work. Last night you left early."

"Eight o'clock."

"Yes, well many of the senior staff put in the
long hours to deal with clients. Last night I had a
very important client that I wanted you to meet.
Mr. Yashida readjusted his schedule to have a
meeting with me because he wants to have a tech-
nology conference here at the end of the year.

Actually his company will be working with the local city government on a project to show how cities from around the world can be partners. It *would've* been a coup if you were able to answer his specific questions."

"I didn't know about this meeting, Mr. Jackson. I would have made arrangements, otherwise."

"I called your house. Since you live in the area, you could've met us at the restaurant. The phone rang out to voice mail."

Haley didn't answer. Her mind raced through the previous evening. Beth had been on the phone in one of her marathon sessions. Her new boss's expression was stern behind his wire-framed glasses.

His receding hairline hardened his features into a gruff exterior that was rarely softened by light-heartedness. The gray in his hair resembled motorcycle handlebars that began from his forehead and swept along the sides over his ears. The hard-nosed salesman seemed to be the only role he knew how to play or embraced with aggression.

"Ms. Sanders, I can't have important meetings like this without you, my conference manager. Otherwise, it's not a meeting, but a social outing. Our expense budget doesn't have the luxury for entertaining potential clients unless a deal is close at hand."

"You said that the city is working with him. I think that means he'll need our expertise to have a successful convention."

"That's not the point, I expect—"

"I've attended all the meetings that you have scheduled late in the evenings and on weekends. I went home past business hours so that I could see my daughter before she went to bed. When I took this job, I made it clear to Mr. Strayer where my priorities stood. I'd be happy to follow up with Mr. Yashida and do whatever needs to be done." Haley hadn't planned to make a speech. She didn't relish a confrontation with her new boss, but she had to set boundaries.

Jackson leaned forward and his chair protested the shift. He planted his elbows on the desk and clasped his hands under his bearded chin. His eyes turned hard and cold. "Mr. Yashida is back in Tokyo." He stood. Haley sensed that Jackson wasn't the type who felt comfortable behind a desk. She raised her chin to meet his intense stare. Although he didn't have the height, he possessed the ability to make his words drip down her spine leaving icicles in their wake. "I spoke up on your behalf when decisions had to be made about your promotion, Ms. Sanders. Remember that."

"Your support is appreciated," she conceded. Maybe she'd defended her position too vigorously. Still, she hadn't said anything that wasn't true.

"Let's move on. What's the status of Bedford's project?"

"Actually I'm meeting with his appointed contact at lunch today. We're all set on our end. Some matters will have to be coordinated between our two offices. One of the major items on our list to discuss is the time line. I'd heard that Bedford may have changes that could affect the logistics."

"Are you sure that you can handle it? This is a big opportunity for us to showcase what this city can do."

"I don't know what you mean." Haley didn't take kindly to any inferences that she couldn't do her job, especially when the job involved tasks that she'd completed as a mere coordinator.

"Maybe I should come with you."

Please don't! She wished that she had the courage to stand up to Jackson. But she'd already gotten on his bad side with her earlier speech. A repeat performance of her work-life balance sentiments might push his patience to the limit.

"Never mind," he said. "Your expression speaks volumes on what you think of my idea. Okay, go do your thing. But when you come back, make sure that you update me." He laughed, his entire girth shaking.

Haley nodded. She definitely counted that as a victory. The first item on her list would be for her to work on hiding her feelings better when dealing with the temperamental Mr. Jackson.

The walk back to her office felt like an ordeal. She badly wanted to get to her small office and close her door. In her new role as manager, however, her attention was in hot demand. Her colleagues stopped her several times in the hallway to get her opinion, respond to her requests or to make a bid for her participation in one of their pet projects.

Playing this political game wore her down. These days she talked so much and met with so many people that she craved quiet and solitude when she got home. To get a bit of downtime, she'd enrolled Beth in an after-school program called the Artists Dream that catered to teens who liked to draw, paint and sketch. Beth had class twice a week to nurture her talent and to give her a positive outlet for her energy.

Giving Beth this chance seemed to help with her mood swings. The atmosphere in the house was calmer, less tense. Haley would settle for their uneasy truce, especially after a long day at work.

The thing she missed the most was Pierce's calls. Since the promotion, she'd come home and fall into bed, only waking up the next day to start her grinding day all over again. She missed hearing his voice at the end of her day. Some romance this was turning out to be.

After the long walk, she was determined to keep her Friday date. Her stress level made it mandatory. Truthfully she needed some good, physical lovemaking to de-stress. She'd read that sex not only helped ease stress, it also burned calories. Her hips could do with a few sexually firming sessions.

Before she could enter her office, Vera hopped up and blocked her entry. Haley looked beyond her assistant's shoulder, wondering if she shielded a visitor.

"Ta da." Vera stepped aside, revealing a vase filled with red, white, yellow and pink roses.

Haley walked over to the flowers and picked up the business-size white card attached to the slender white ribbon around the vase. Even without the flowers, the vase had to be expensive with its exquisite cut and intricate design.

The note read: *Friday!*

"So who's it from?" Vera strained her neck to see the card. Her big hair partially blocked Haley's view.

Haley pushed the card back in the envelope and stuck it in her pocket. Vera did her job like a high-performance employee, a wonderful asset to her team. But her assistant had to be kept within a defined area that couldn't breach her personal life. Unless she wanted the entire office and a few unrelated residents of the office complex to know her business, her love life had to be kept deep in the closet.

Pierce's thoughtfulness pleased her. How had he accurately read her mind? Perhaps because he'd had trouble getting in touch with her, he'd guessed that she was backing out. Writing the one key word on the card and sending it hand delivered, with flowers in tow, made it difficult for

An Important Message from the Publisher

Dear Reader,

Because you've chosen to read one of our fine novels, I'd like to say "thank you"! And, as a special way to say thank you, I'm offering to send you two more Kimani Romance novels and two surprise gifts – absolutely FREE! These books will keep it real with true-to-life African American characters that turn up the heat and sizzle with passion.

Please enjoy the free books and gifts with our compliments...

Linda Gill

Publisher, Kimani Press

Peel off Seal and Place Inside...

THE EDITOR'S "THANK YOU" FREE GIFTS INCLUDE:

▶ Two NEW Kimani Romance™ Novels

▶ Two exciting surprise gifts

YES! I have placed my Editor's "thank you" Free Gifts seal in the space provided at right. Please send me 2 FREE books, and my 2 FREE Mystery Gifts. I understand that I am under no obligation to purchase anything further, as explained on the back of this card.

PLACE FREE GIFTS SEAL HERE

▼ DETACH AND MAIL CARD TODAY! ▼

168 XDL EF2F

368 XDL EF2R

FIRST NAME	LAST NAME

ADDRESS

APT.#	CITY

STATE/PROV.	ZIP/POSTAL CODE

Thank You!

(K-ROM-09/06)

The Reader Service — Here's How It Works:

If offer card is missing write to: The Reader Service, 3010 Walden Ave., P.O. Box 1867, Buffalo, NY 14240-1867

BUSINESS REPLY MAIL
FIRST-CLASS MAIL   PERMIT NO. 717-003   BUFFALO, NY

POSTAGE WILL BE PAID BY ADDRESSEE

THE READER SERVICE
3010 WALDEN AVE
PO BOX 1867
BUFFALO NY 14240-9952

NO POSTAGE
NECESSARY
IF MAILED
IN THE
UNITED STATES

her to change her mind. If he only knew she wanted him too much to back out of their date.

"I'll take them and put the little packet of flower preserve in the water." Vera took the flowers, ready to bury her face in the bunch. Haley wasn't in the mood to share. "Thanks, but I've got it." She ushered Vera out of her office. She closed the door and set down the heavy vase. In the privacy of her office, she touched each rose, running her cheek over the soft petals, before bending close to inhale their sweet, heady scent.

Pierce had not only surprised her, but lifted her spirits after that energy-sucking, exhaustion-induced meeting with Jackson. She wished that she could see him at this very minute. She was liable to jump into his arms and kiss him until his legs gave out from her weight.

An hour later, she and Mr. Hopkins had coordinated their lunch meeting at the Caribbean hangout located on Restaurant Row. The road was aptly named for the ten restaurants that lined either side. It wasn't her first choice for a meeting, since she would have to yell to be heard over the din of the lunchtime crowd. But she'd yield to the client's wishes. It was a small price to pay.

The restaurant had a policy not to seat anyone

until everyone in the party was present. Arriving early earned Haley a spot in the outer waiting area of the busy restaurant. Thankfully her client arrived within a minute of their meeting time. His timing was perfect.

Pierce always had lunch once or twice a month with his mentor, Morton Bell. Dr. Bell was renowned in his field of ophthalmology, but had earned higher respect for his philanthropic endeavors. The older man had taught Pierce for several of his university courses. After failing his first test in anatomy, Pierce had visited him in the crammed university office to plead his case for a better grade. The professor had been deaf to his pleas for mercy. After a stern lecture, Pierce had buckled down, learning not to overestimate his grasp of the curriculum.

From that point, Pierce had become a frequent visitor to the professor's office. He'd liked to think that his intriguing questions and dedication to the class had placed him in good stead with Morton. Knowing Morton, Pierce suspected that his professor might have thought that Pierce idolized Morton more as a father figure than as a mentor.

This month they met in a local Caribbean restaurant. The lunch crowd was young and noisy. At least with the universities back in session, the place wasn't as crowded with college students.

Pierce didn't mind the lively discussions or the young people. He could picture his brother seated at one of the tables trying to sound mature and knowledgeable without any money in his pocket. Their carefree attitudes amused Pierce. Besides, Morton had chosen the place because of the younger generation. He claimed that he liked to observe the future.

"What's been going on? You've cancelled on me twice. Thought you'd finally met someone," Morton said and stroked his beard, chuckling at his remark. Pierce always thought the professor looked like the actor Samuel Jackson.

"Keep dreaming. I'm born to be the bachelor and I've never wanted to take the dive to despair of marriage."

Morton waved his words away. "You're pretty melancholy. Take a minute to soak up the sunshine. Maybe it'll bring you a better disposition. Perhaps you're down on marriage because you still can't find someone who wants to be with you?"

"See, that's where you're wrong. I do have a wonderful friend. As a matter of fact, we're going out tomorrow."

Their food arrived, delaying Morton's reply. Pierce saw the gleam in his eyes. The questions formulating in his mind practically leaped off the older man's face.

Pierce had a salad topped with curried chicken breast. The curry didn't burn his tongue, but added enough spice to make him reach for his water glass. Morton had ignored the ethnic food and ordered a large hamburger and coleslaw. He had to stretch his mouth to encompass the large sandwich.

"I'm waiting." Morton set down his sandwich; more than a bite-size mouthful poked out the side of his cheek.

Pierce filled him in on Haley in general, and specifically, how beautiful and marvelous she was, including how much Beth had grown on him. With any other friend, he would have concentrated on keeping any personal, subjective comments out of the conversation. However with Morton, he wanted to tell him everything about Haley.

"My, but it sure looks like someone may be in love."

"Don't know if I'd go that far. But that's not what makes a relationship survive. Love is a good thing to have, but you need someone who would stick through the thick and thin."

"Most people plan to do that anyway. No one goes into a relationship saying I hope it will fail."

"But when there are signs, they bail out. Their actions speak louder than what they say." Pierce hated talking about relationships. It was up there with talking about politics and religion. Some people were advocates, some weren't. He was ambivalent. As long as Haley didn't push the subject with him, they would be fine.

"Let's switch to a subject that won't make you bare your teeth. How's your family?" Morton asked.

"Sheena is Sheena. She is mad at me because I want to sell Mom's house. I'm not paying her any mind."

"Does she want the house?"

"No, and that's my point," Pierce said.

"Did you ask her?" Morton looked at him, shaking his head.

"Don't you start. She already has a house. Why should I ask her?"

"The house belongs to the entire family. You

controlled the estate, but they have an emotional tie to the house that you've ignored," Morton said.

"I'm selling it to Haley."

"The same Haley? Does Sheena know about you and the tenant getting it on?" Morton wiped his mouth. "This is getting good."

"I don't know if Sheena knows. I'm sure Laura has briefed her by now, but it doesn't matter. I should've cancelled this lunch with you," Pierce muttered. He finished off his salad, spearing the last piece of chicken. Morton, who was lagging behind Pierce, dug into his food with relish.

"What about Laura?"

"Laura, thank goodness, has come around to my side. She likes Haley and spends time with Beth." He couldn't help the gloat in his voice.

"Beth is the daughter, right? Ready-made family, all neatly packaged up for you."

"Beth is still adjusting to her parents' breakup. Remember how long it took for me to get over it."

"And still getting over it. You're hanging on to the memories like it's a life raft. If you let go, you'd be fine. You'd stand on those large feet of yours and be just fine."

"Back to Beth—she painted the mural in my office."

"The psychedelic-looking wall at your office?"

"I'm allowing someone's creative juice to breathe. And my patients could do with some cheeriness while they wait."

"Sounds like making Beth happy was more the priority than your patients. Nothing wrong with that, but once you're in with kids, you'd better plan to stay in."

Pierce heard the warning in Morton's message. He would never use Beth's feelings to manipulate the situation between her mother and him. All he'd done was provide a solution when she'd needed one.

He couldn't say that he wasn't glad Laura had made some inroads with Beth. Haley had been worried about the close friendship between Laura and Beth. Haley wanted to be the one who Beth turned to for advice. But Laura had made it clear that she wouldn't keep anything from Haley. Haley, in return, had promised that she would think before reacting to information Laura shared with her about Beth.

"I mustn't forget Omar. What has become of the dreamer?"

"He's studying for the LSAT. He took it once, but I advised him to start studying again, just in case."

"A lawyer, very prestigious. Is this a career race between brothers?"

"Considering that I'm already a doctor, the race is purely one-sided."

"Why don't you talk him out of it?"

"He needs to do something logical and lucrative. I can't take care of him for the rest of his life. And our sisters shouldn't be helping him, although I know they do. He's a young man and it's time for him to stand on his own two feet."

"Isn't he already working? As a teacher?" Morton raised an eyebrow, chewing on his last fry.

"Part-time. With budget cuts, he may be out of a job."

"Lawyers get laid off, too."

"Morton, are you here to stomp on my nerves? In your family, you've got an ophthalmologist, a plastic surgeon and an obstetrician. Why can't I want the same standard for my family?"

"Each of us picked our career. My father owned a dry-cleaning business and a grocery store. Life wasn't a walk in the park because we were expected to carry on the business. My father felt that he'd put all this work into the business as a legacy of sorts for us. When each of his children selected a career in the medical field, he got frustrated and sold the family business. He gave us each a nest egg and wished us luck when he retired," Morton said as he sat back, folding his arms across his chest. "Give your sisters and brother a chance. They won't disappoint you."

"Maybe."

"Expect the worst from people and they will oblige…" Morton's voice trailed off, his attention diverted. Pierce knew Morton was about to launch into a full-blown lecture that would leave him rethinking everything in his life.

"What shut you up? Or should I ask *who* did?" Pierce laughed at his friend, knowing that some young thing had caught Morton's eye. The older man had lost his wife five years before to a terminal illness. His friend still mourned and wore a cavalier, flirtatious attitude to hide his grief. Pierce could identify with that approach.

Morton pointed toward the door. "The sister with the killer blue suit. Forget the dude. She looks like she could eat nails for breakfast and still look sexy in some fishnet stockings. I love a strong woman." Morton returned his attention to Pierce. "Is Haley a strong woman? Frankly I can't see you being happy with anyone less."

"After what you said, I don't think that I should be talking about Haley to you. Now you're into fishnet stockings? You are sinking into the den of iniquity pretty quickly." Pierce craned his neck to see who had rendered Morton speechless. The woman either had left or had been seated in a booth. "Haley is a strong, stubborn, sophisticated, savvy, sexy woman." He couldn't help bragging.

"I think that's as close as we'll get for poetry from you. Next thing I know you'll be dancing and singing, while strumming on a mandolin while you serenade the fair-headed Haley."

"Actually her hair is a soft brown."

"There she is," Morton whispered, loud enough for the man accompanying the woman to turn and stare at them. "She's looking over here. Oh, this is sweet. I think she's ditching the bald-headed dude to join us. Move over, Pierce."

Pierce finally saw the woman who had Morton blithering. He was surprised to see Haley, but his male ego preened that his woman turned heads. Pierce held his face straight.

"Hi there," Haley said and greeted each man with a smile. "This is a nice surprise."

Pierce stood and kissed her cheek. Was this how good she looked when she went to work?

He'd love the chance to be able to see her every morning.

"Haley, I hope?" Morton shook her hand, but didn't let go. Haley nodded. "I'm Pierce's mentor. I tell him all the things that he should be doing. I take complete credit for all of his good points."

"Well, you've done a heck of a job." Haley touched Pierce's cheek, her face filled with tenderness. "I've got to get back to my lunch meeting."

"Pierce Masterson, you lucky dog. I can't believe that a woman of her caliber is interested in you," Morton said with a teasing chuckle. Morton reached for his glass and finished drinking his beverage. He wiped his lips with a flourish. "You will be inviting me over to meet her and really get to know her, right?"

"Never. I don't want you filling her head with any nonsense." Pierce had thought about introducing Haley to the rest of his family and friends. But he didn't know how she would feel about meeting them. She seemed to be keeping him at a distance.

"I promise to keep a beer in my hand. Every time I get an urge to say something that might embarrass you, I'll take a drink."

"Great. You can be obnoxious and inebriated. Can't wait for that scenario to play out."

"Seriously, though, Pierce, both of you may be tiptoeing through the tulips. I'm an outsider and I can look at your relationship objectively. Both of you are smitten with each other. Stop fighting it. Let things happen without your crazy reservations intervening."

Pierce heard the words, the underlying meaning, all the nuances to Morton's philosophy. He wished that he could truly be impulsive as he had once bragged to Haley. Instead, he pondered and made his moves with great caution.

Morton pulled out his cell phone. He dialed a number and placed the phone to his ear. He winked at Pierce and made a motion to remain quiet while he talked.

"Sheena, sweetheart, it's Morton Bell, husband number two when husband number one doesn't work out." He laughed.

Pierce wished that he could hear his sister's comments to Morton. Based on his responses, he was getting clarity on Sheena's version of things. He could feel another lecture coming on after this telephone conversation.

"I'd love to come to dinner. By the way, I ran

into your brother and his friend Haley. He said that you're having a cookout. Heard that you always have a barbeque on the last Saturday of the summer to celebrate the end of season."

Pierce made a motion to cut off the mention of Haley. Morton smiled, but kept talking. "Yes, that Haley. Okay, I'll see you then." Morton hung up.

"Have you lost your mind? I'm not taking Haley over to Sheena. If you had waited a few minutes, I was going to mention that I am having a small gathering over at my house this Saturday."

"You can still do it. I'd love to come and get to know your intended."

"See, that's why I don't want you near her."

"What time?" Morton ignored Pierce's protests.

"How about three o'clock in the afternoon."

"Good. I'll be over on Saturday at three." Morton looked at his watch. "I have to get moving. I've got a three o'clock tee time this afternoon. An opthamologist's life is so decadent. Told you to go that route." Morton grinned. He patted Pierce on his back. "Good luck. See you Saturday. And don't try to cancel, I'll still show up. Now why don't you leave me and go talk to her. She must be wrapping up her meeting soon."

"Yeah." Pierce didn't take his eyes off Haley.

"You've got the love bug in a bad way. Later, my friend." Pierce heard Morton's chuckle as he left the restaurant.

Pierce moved to Morton's seat to get an unobstructed view of Haley and her lunch companion. He choked on the thought of the well-dressed man as Haley's date. After three refills of his soda, Haley finally had finished her lunch. Being a doctor and having to observe people and their body language to make a quick diagnosis, Pierce had formed an opinion of Haley's companion before the man left her table. Like Morton, this man had fallen under Haley's spell.

Pierce found Haley's lunch "date's" rapt attention quite annoying. The man hung on every word she said. If he thought that Haley wouldn't be furious, he would have parked his butt at the table. The man had the look of a stuffed suit. He probably didn't do anything meaningful but count his dough. Haley appeared to be unaffected, taking notes whenever the man spoke. Once she looked up and caught Pierce's stare.

He looked down at his glass, suddenly interested in the ice cube that was shaped like a mountain. When he thought enough time had passed, he looked up to see that the meeting was over. Haley shook the man's hand. As they stood, he stopped to ask her something. Was he asking for her phone number? Haley shook her head. The man shrugged, smiled and walked out of the restaurant. Pierce toasted his last gulp of drink to Haley.

She didn't approach him, as he'd expected. Instead, she also exited the restaurant. He got up, bumping back his chair with a loud scrape along the floor. Dodging other patrons and waiters bearing heavy trays of food, he got to the door and flung it open.

She had crossed the parking lot, heading for her car. He ran out, jumping aside when an irritated driver honked at him.

"Haley, wait."

"Finished spying on me?"

Pierce slowed his steps. He didn't mean to anger her. She certainly did look cross. Maybe he had overdone his stalker routine. "Don't be mad at me."

"I'm not. I think that you're comical. Do I get to come and look at you tend to your patients?"

"Just making sure that Mr. Corporate Suit didn't get fresh."

"Fresh?" Haley laughed.

"I swear he was making goo-goo eyes at you."

"You jealous man. I'll give you a chance to make it up to me."

"Really?" Pierce could only think of one way. His way required both of them to be lying in the same bed…naked.

"I know what you're thinking. And that's not it."

"Darn it."

"Go back to work, Pierce."

"Right. Right." Pierce wasn't ready to let her go, but he couldn't very well hold her hostage in the restaurant parking lot.

Chapter 8

Pierce went back to work with a smile on his face. His mood had been boosted by the unexpected meeting with Haley. Even his patients complimented him on his upbeat demeanor, attributing their improved attitude to it when they left his office.

"Jean, did you send out the invitations?"

"Yep. I sent out an invitation to everyone. So far, we have fifty that are definite and twelve that can't make it. Are you sure we can handle fifty guests?"

"We'll have to make sure to stagger the refreshments to accommodate all of the guests at the open house. Don't put out everything at one time, or the early birds will eat it all."

Jean gathered the papers on her desk and sorted them into a pile. She paused in her task and looked up at him.

"What?"

"You're doing an awfully nice thing for that kid."

"She's got talent. So why not show it off?"

"Yeah, but most people would have looked the other way. Frankly, I was scared for her when I saw how she and her friends had defaced the fence."

"Believe me, I was mad. That wasn't an act," he said. He recalled how defeated Haley had looked by what Beth had done. Guess he did it for the mother, as much as he'd done it for the daughter.

"Does Beth know about the party?"

He shook his head. "I haven't told her yet. Maybe that's what I'll do tonight."

"I'm going to get out of here, Doc. I'll see you tomorrow."

Jean had given him an idea about the event.

Announcing the event to Haley and Beth provided him with the perfect excuse to visit them. As he locked up the office, he whistled at the prospect of his new mission. Once he slid the key into the lock, he paused. He reopened the door, glancing down at the object that had nagged him.

Beth had left her red-and-black backpack during her last painting session. He'd put the bag in his office for safekeeping. He went back into the office and retrieved the bag. Now with the backpack slung over his shoulder, his whistle turned into singing as he closed up the office. Another practical reason for a visit had presented itself. He had to stop at Haley's to return Beth's bag.

He never got to see Haley on weeknights. She came home late and besides, she felt guilty about not dedicating more time to Beth. He couldn't argue with that. He didn't want to usurp the precious time Haley spent with her daughter.

Visiting Haley and Beth was enough for him. He didn't require major conversation or a three-course dinner. Sitting on the porch sharing a bowl of ice cream with Haley and Beth would satisfy him.

When he emerged from his office, night had

already fallen. The streets were wet. He must have missed a late afternoon downpour. Traffic was still a little heavy. The noisy whish of tires on the wet asphalt filled the air. He merged into the traffic, adding to the many drivers heading home, only he wasn't going to his house.

No matter how many times he came to visit Haley or do work on the house, he never stopped admiring his family home. The front porch was wide and inviting, a reminder of times when families spent after-dinner hours chatting with each other without leaving their yards. The porch had been his perch when his siblings rode their bikes or roller skates up and down the street. The porch had provided him with a clear view, and he'd had the added benefit of neighbors who would tell him what his siblings were doing at the end of the road.

Haley had planted flowers along the stone path, as his mother had done. He didn't pretend to know anything about gardening. After his mother had died, he hadn't tended them. His sisters hadn't, either. He suspected that they didn't want to disturb something that their mother had last touched. Their mother's garden had eventually withered and died.

He rang the doorbell, hoping that at this late hour Haley was home. A curtain was pulled back and Beth peered out the window at him. She waved, then disappeared from view. Moments later, the locks were released and the door opened wide.

"Hey, Doc, Mom's in the back cooking, I think."

"And you're helping?"

"No, sir. I'm—" Beth motioned to the couch where thick textbooks lay open "—I'm doing my homework."

He followed her in and picked up one of the books. "Pre-calculus?" He made a motion of bowing to her. "Who knew?"

Beth blushed. "My teacher wanted to challenge me. I have ten problems to complete."

"I hope you don't need help."

"Naw, I'm cool." Beth laughed.

Pierce wanted to encourage her to do that more often. A smile transformed her face. But one wrong move or statement and he knew that she could revert to her usual adolescent scowl.

"Looks like you've got something for me," she said.

"You left this at my office. Thought you may need something in it for school," he said.

"Thanks. I didn't need it though. That's not my homework backpack." She shook her head at the object and then at him.

"Should I say—'loser' because I can see it written all over your face." Beth hooted. Now he understood. As long as he placed himself in a ridiculous situation or poked fun at himself, she didn't mind his company.

"Doc, I don't use a backpack. Figured since you're the doctor, you'd know that the device isn't good for the back, especially the way kids wear it slung over one shoulder."

"Cut me a break, kid, or I won't tell you my other surprise." He had to regain the upper hand in the situation.

"Beth? Who was that?" Haley asked as she came into the room.

Pierce looked up to see Haley come down the stairs. He saw her bare feet then her ankle and the hemline of a thick terry robe as she descended. When she caught sight of him, she froze on the steps. Her head was wrapped in a bright yellow towel that didn't in any way detract from her beauty. All he could do was gulp in air and hope that his voice would return.

"Oh, Pierce, I didn't expect to see you…in my living room. Is something the matter?" Her fingers clutched the robe and the other hand patted the towel.

"Sorry for the intrusion." The mannerly thing to do would've been to call ahead. He'd been too caught up in his motives to consider the effects of dropping in on Haley unannounced.

"No, it's all right. Have a seat. Excuse me for a minute."

She disappeared back up the stairs. He shifted his attention back to Beth, who had resumed her homework. He sat across from her, and looked at the framed photographs that captured Beth's and Haley's past. Haley in the eighties not only held his interest, but caused him to burst into laughter. She wore a pantsuit that had faux leather trim. Her shoulders cut sharp right angles with shoulder pads large enough to protect a line-backer. And her hair stood a good three inches above her head with flips on either side. The complete look had him doubled over with laughter. And yet, no matter how bizarre her attire, Haley still radiated a natural beauty.

Pierce stood. He really shouldn't have dropped in. Haley hadn't come down and Beth had her work to complete. "Beth, please tell your mom that I didn't mean to intrude. I was only returning the bag."

"Mom!"

Pierce cringed at the high-pitched scream from the bony young girl.

Haley emerged in a black T-shirt and black jeans. The simple attire looked like a million dollars on her body. Her hair, still damp, framed her face in loose waves. She wore no makeup. It wasn't necessary.

"Were you leaving? Sorry I took so long. Please, stay. Would you like something to drink?" Haley prayed that he would step away from the door, back into her tiny living room.

First, she had been shocked to see his large frame dwarfing her room. But that had only been an instant reaction. She couldn't deny the happiness she felt when he smiled at her.

"Actually, I had an appointment this evening. Thankfully it was rescheduled. I got to come home and pamper myself for a few minutes." She walked over and placed a hand on Beth's shoulder. "How's the homework coming?"

"I'm finished." Beth snapped the book closed. "I'll set the table for dinner."

"Thanks, sweetheart. Pierce, have you eaten dinner?"

He shook his head.

"Good."

"Beth, can you set a spot for Pierce?"

"Don't go to any trouble. Show me where it is and I'll do it."

"You're the guest, Doc. I know this used to be your house, but you have to act like a guest when you're here." Beth was busy adding more utensils to the table.

"I've been duly chastised. Thank you."

Haley felt the blood rush to her face. She knew from Beth's voice that she wasn't being mean-spirited. But she had to realize that there was a fine line with rudeness. Pierce winked at her.

"Don't let her push your buttons," he whispered low enough for her ears only. "I know that I'm imposing, but after seeing you at lunch, I wanted to see you again. Besides, I had a legitimate excuse."

"Really?" She folded her arms, measuring his demeanor for honesty.

Pierce pointed to the backpack. She got up and

inspected it, vaguely remembering when she'd bought it for Beth.

"Let's go eat. Don't get your hopes up, though. It's only baked chicken, stuffing and spinach."

"It's more than I would have eaten tonight. I think that I've a peanut-butter-and-jelly sandwich with my name on it at home."

"You're such a bachelor. You only cook when seduction is on the menu?"

"Something like that."

"I hope that your kitchen doesn't get much use."

"It didn't until a woman and her daughter landed on my doorstep."

The microwave buzzed. "Looks like Beth nuked our dinner. Hopefully it's not rubber chicken."

They shared a laugh as they walked over to the table. Beth had placed herself at the head of the table with Pierce and her mother sitting opposite each other at the sides. Haley studied her daughter's face for any signs that this was a joke. Beth looked innocently back at her and then at Pierce before taking her seat.

They ate dinner and conversed about the day's events. Beth lit up when it was her turn to talk about her day. Haley wanted to hug Pierce for taking the time to ask questions about Beth's work and friends at school. Beth's easy chatter with him revealed things that Haley didn't know about Beth's likes and dislikes.

Listening to Beth made her realize that she had to keep a line of communication open or she would be locked out of her daughter's life. Not everything required her input or even reaction, but she needed time to talk to her.

"Doc said he had something to tell me. What is it?" Beth pushed.

Haley looked at Pierce, wondering what else he could be up to. "I'm all ears."

"I came to tell you about my open house." He held up his finger. "Hold on. Both of you are so impatient. I'm having the party so that we can unveil Beth's wall mural."

"Oh, wow! Mom, can you believe that everyone will see my wall painting?" Beth bounced in her seat.

Haley saw her daughter's indecision on whether to sit there and continue the conversation or run from the table and call her friends. Haley decided to make it easy for her. She nodded to Beth, letting her escape.

"You're the greatest, Doc." Beth hugged Pierce before running to the phone.

Pierce stared after Beth, then looked at Haley.

"Don't question it. I've learned to go with whatever comes. Beth's mood swings certainly keeps our lives fresh," she said.

"I'm touched."

Pierce didn't need to tell her that he had been affected by Beth's acknowledgment of what he'd done for her. His face had softened. His mouth twitched into a ready smile. His genuine affection for her daughter was reflected in his face.

They cleaned up the dining room in a matter of minutes.

"Meet you on the porch?"

"Sure. I'll run up for my Afghan throw," she said.

Haley pulled the lightweight blanket from the linen closet. She treasured the rare evenings they spent together on the porch, sitting side by side sharing ice cream talking about the day's accomplishments or frustrations. Pierce and his fine physique could eat the ice cream and be unaffected. She, on the other hand, alternated the treats with fresh fruit and frozen yogurt.

Ever since their ill-fated assignation that had ended prematurely, Haley hadn't encouraged Pierce to come over, even for the nightly treats.

Beth's reaction to the turn in their relationship worried her. The less Pierce visited, the more sullen Beth became. She couldn't blame all of the tension in the house on Beth. More of the blame lay squarely at her feet as she played tug-of-war with her emotions and her attention to the good doctor.

Pierce was already on the porch when Haley came downstairs. Beth was still on the phone. She overheard her giving directions to Pierce's office. Haley hoped he had a hefty food budget for the open house. He would have to have plenty of goodies on hand to feed all of Beth's friends. She gave Beth a hand signal to wrap up the phone call. She knew it would take at least two more warnings before Beth hung up. She sighed; it was their nightly ritual.

"Mad at me for dropping in?" Pierce patted the spot next to him on the wicker love seat.

Haley shook her head. She kicked off her shoes and slipped her feet under the blanket. A soft sigh escaped her lips. Sitting on the porch had become a wonderful way for her to de-stress. The stained wood with white rails had a quaint country feel while sitting in a very modern city. Her position on the wicker chair she'd recently splurged on made her feel as if she were between two worlds, her hectic job and life.

On most days, this was her favorite spot, an oasis where she could regroup. She breathed in the air, loving the fresh scent after a hearty rainfall. The thick rain clouds had cleared, revealing an inky-blue sky peppered with twinkling stars. The crescent eggshell-white moon stood in stark contrast against the dark backdrop of the heavens.

Haley kept staring up at the sky as she did on the nights that she sat with Pierce, hoping to see a shooting star. She hadn't formed her wish. Her thoughts were like fragments circling around in her mind and inspired by her heart. One name sat at the edge of her lips, waiting for the night when a star would race across the sky. Sending his name out into the universe was enough, she believed. All her dreams, cares, fantasies would follow his name to the twinkling star.

"How about a special treat tonight." Pierce presented her with a chocolate ice-cream bar.

"Oh, you're going the decadent route," Haley said and pounced on her gift. She ripped open the wrapper, with no desire to read the nutrition label. There was nothing like a dark chocolate treat.

Her hand and mouth coordinated on autopilot. She rolled her eyes as the ice cream melted onto her tongue, before closing her mouth to savor the stimulation to her senses.

"If I'd known you were going to have an erotic reaction, I would have held on to it for black-mailing purposes."

"How did you know that this was the only thing in the world that would make me feel better? I'm a sucker for chocolate."

"I'm not sure where that leaves me?"

She kissed him, leaving a chocolate imprint near his lips, and resumed eating her treat. "Can't let it melt. Give me a second."

Haley didn't care how she looked gobbling her dessert. Pierce offered her several napkins and laid them on her lap and chest in a sincere effort to save her clothes and blanket.

"Stop smiling at me. Chocolate around those pearly whites is not a pleasant sight." He pulled her into his arms and seared her with a bawdy kiss. "I'm beginning to feel lonely sitting here keeping myself company."

"Now you know that you can't give me an ice-cream Popsicle and expect conversation."

"There won't be any of this on Friday." He

kissed her temple as she rested her head against his shoulder. "I'll have to throw out the entire box."

"Yeah, Friday." She really did try to make her voice sound upbeat and excited. When he leaned forward to study her face, she knew that she'd failed.

"Talk to me, Haley," he urged.

She followed his gaze out onto the road leading to the main intersection. How could she tell him that Friday, Friday night, Saturday morning would all be major, gigantic steps for her. Her breathing became labored just thinking about it.

Their impromptu plan the other day hadn't caused her advisory lights to flash. His invitation and her acceptance had been spontaneous. She knew that her daughter's discovery stood at the core of their impulsiveness.

"I want you to understand how difficult all of this is for me. I'm not sure that I'm ready for this weekend."

"It's one night." He held her gaze until she looked away and then righted herself in the chair. "Look, I don't want to sound like the horny boyfriend pushing you to do something that you'd rather not do, but I need to know what is bothering you. One time, I think that it's Beth dealing with us being more than friends. At another time, I think it's you being afraid to open up and care about someone." He ran his hand over his head. She heard his frustrated sigh before he turned his head away from her. "Sometimes I even think that I'm the problem. That I'm not good enough for you. I'm not talking about professionally or financially. I wonder if I measure up to what you consider to be an ideal man."

"You have always been thoughtful and sweet to me and Beth. How can you not be the ideal man? My heart is touched with your sensitivity," she said and realized that she sounded like a greeting card. "Look, Pierce, I don't know if I should be doing this right now. I'm not talking about Beth, I'm talking about me. I'm the one with the problem. I don't want you to think that I can't function without you. Or that I'm needy. From the first day that we met you came to Beth's rescue and you continue to do so." She stopped talking, unsure how to tell him how insecure she felt.

"Friday is two days away. Let's not cancel. If you're there on Friday, I'll know that you're ready to move on with me." He didn't wait for her reply.

He took his bowl and spoon and walked into the kitchen, then came out on the porch where she still remained. "Good night." He walked down the steps without their traditional nose rub and kiss.

Haley looked at his car through the rails of the porch. She hadn't moved a muscle since he'd last spoken. Pierce had not only tossed the ball into her court, he'd handed her the racket.

Pierce parked in front of Sheena's house. Tired of their rift, he'd called her. She hadn't said that she didn't want to see him, and he'd taken that as a good sign. They could talk about the weather. They could talk about the latest high-school football game. The topic of conversation didn't really matter. He simply missed being around his family, all of them.

Plus he wanted the family, especially Sheena, to visit on Saturday. Haley's visit, if she showed up, would remain his secret surprise. But if she backed out, he would have his family to help him get through the disappointment. Not that he would give up on Haley. Too much had passed between them and there was that small fact that he couldn't deny. She had found a way into his heart, Pierce admitted grudgingly.

Sheena appeared from the backyard. His sister who was very fashion conscious looked disheveled. An orange scarf secured her hair. Brown gardening gloves covered her hands. Her face had brown smudges to match the dirty fingers of her gloves. Gone were the bright reds and blues that she wore as her signature colors. She didn't usually wear a T-shirt, denim shorts and ratty tennis shoes. Sheena beckoned to him. He waved and hurried to catch up with her retreating figure.

"What's all this?" Pierce surveyed the backyard that looked as if someone had turned it inside out. The enclosed space had a series of deep trenches, piles of dirt, stacks of lumber and a backhoe parked under a tree.

"I'm rebuilding the deck over here and building a bigger deck up there." Sheena first pointed at the family room on ground level and then up to the deck off the dining room. "I was trying to save some of the plants that lined the area."

"Didn't know you had it in you." Pierce couldn't hide his surprise. Seeing Sheena in this setting opened his eyes. Looking at Sheena, he realized how much she'd matured into a loving wife and mother. No longer did she fit neatly into the category of malleable little sister.

"Come over here." Sheena pulled him to another area of the yard where the earth had been dug up.

"Burying the family?" He elbowed her, which she promptly returned with a jab to his stomach.

"Inground pool."

Pierce choked. "Are you sure that you can manage such an expense? A pool and all these other renovations only make sense if you're planning to make this your dream house."

Sheena shook her head. She threw up her hands and screamed through clenched teeth. She pulled off her gloves and stalked off toward the house.

"What's the problem?" he asked, although he had caught himself a little too late. Maybe he could play the dumb role and beg for her mercy.

At least she hadn't locked the door, he thought, as he followed her into the family room. The renovations weren't just outdoors. The family-room walls were now a tropical green with decorations that made the room look like an island getaway. Looking out the doors to the backyard, his imagination filled in the space with the deck and the pool.

"I think this is going to be awesome." Pierce really admired what Sheena had done. "I'm sorry for jumping all over you a few minutes ago."

"It's getting old, Pierce. You always jump on anything that I want to do that doesn't involve you." Sheena stood next to him. "Carlton and I decided that we're comfortable in this house. We've got enough room. Instead of splurging on a big, new house and skimpy yard in another neighborhood, we can make this house and our backyard into what we want."

Pierce heard her logic. "You grew up on me, and I don't know if I can handle it," he said.

Sheena rubbed his back. "There will be times when I'll need you, big brother, but for the most part I can handle my life. I don't need rescuing. Don't forget I now have a husband who is my shining knight. He's my number-one guy, Pierce."

No translation was necessary. Her message came through with a clarity that made his stomach clench.

"Staying for dinner? Maybe you can tell me about your tenant. Morton was gushing about her," Sheena said as they headed upstairs to the kitchen.

"Sure," Pierce said, realizing that he wasn't

ready to tell her about Haley. From the way she mentioned Morton's "gushing," he'd refrain from making any comments about her. "Where's Carlton, senior and junior?"

"Carlton took Junior to visit his mother. They'll be back sometime this evening," she explained.

"Why don't I keep you company till they get back," he said. Standing in her kitchen, he realized that he did miss Sheena's former open-door policy. Although he'd eaten an hour ago, he wouldn't pass up the opportunity to sit and chat and even laugh with his younger sister.

"I'll fix some leftovers, but you need to get out of my way. You're hovering," Sheena said and playfully pushed him away.

"Fine. I'm better off on the sidelines. And besides, you're trampling on my ego pretty good." Pierce grabbed a banana from the bowl on the counter.

"You're going to ruin your appetite," Sheena said as she pulled three thick pieces of pork chops from the oven. "Potato salad?"

Pierce nodded and tossed the banana peel into the trash. "Sheena, I really want to talk about the house. I feel as if it still stands between us. We've never had anything of this magnitude between us."

Sheena put down his plate and set another spot at the table before she took her place.

"Who's joining us?"

"Omar." She pointed her fork at him. "When he gets here, don't jump on him."

Pierce didn't respond. Several questions were ready to spill off his tongue. He hadn't seen Omar in weeks. Obviously, Omar was still in Sheena's good graces.

"I mean it, Pierce. You can't run his life," she continued.

"Sounds like you've taken up that baton." He shoved a piece of pork chop into his mouth. So what if he sounded jealous. "For some reason, you all see me as the big bad guy who has ruined your lives."

The front door opened and Omar breezed in. The way he moved would make people think that he was a serious athlete.

"Yo, sis." Omar's greeting died when he walked into the dining room. "Hey, Pierce," he said and nodded in Pierce's direction. Omar didn't smile or grin in greeting.

"Omar." Pierce swallowed the questions that

he wanted to pour down his brother's throat. If he went down that route, Sheena would be all over him. As much as he acted as if he didn't care what they thought, he didn't enjoy being alone in an emotional corner with none of his siblings on his side.

"Something wrong?" Omar looked at Sheena, then cautiously at Pierce.

"No," Pierce answered. "I dropped by and wanted to invite you all over on Saturday afternoon. Nothing big. Mainly family and close friends. I think Morton will be there." If Omar refused to talk to him about something as important as his future, he knew that Morton would take the younger Masterson male under his wing the same way he'd mentored Pierce.

"Inviting your tenant and her daughter?" Sheena asked, turning her keen gaze on him.

"Laura will be hanging out with Beth. They're heading to West Virginia on a shopping trip that had to be cut short when Laura got sick the other day."

"Haven't talked to Laura lately. She said that she had the stomach flu," Sheena added.

"She was down for about two days. I told her to keep drinking liquids even when she didn't feel like eating." Pierce looked at the plate with more than half of his food untouched. His stomach threatened to bust. "I believe she's feeling better," Pierce concluded.

"Are you done?" Omar asked, eyeing Pierce's plate. Pierce shoved his meal toward Omar. Food around Omar never went to waste.

"You've talked about the daughter. What about the mother?"

Pierce knew he had stepped onto a marshy area from the frosty nip in Sheena's voice. However, she hadn't met Haley. Any bias against Haley circled back to the house that happened to be at the center of every issue.

"I've invited Haley. If she can make it, you and Omar can meet her."

"Hold everything, you're getting it on with the tenant? And she's got a child!" Omar set his knife down and held up his hand for a high five with Pierce. "You da man, big brother," Omar crowed.

Pierce could have used this moment as a chance to bond with his younger brother. He could have shown that he was down like that, and all the other hip slang he could think of. But slapping palms over his woman wasn't "cool" or respectful.

Omar lowered his hand when Pierce sat back

in the chair, his hands firmly set on the table. Omar's silly grin quickly evaporated.

"Glad I'm not the only one that has a problem with this," Sheena prompted.

"I don't know why that is, Sheena. As the landlord, I've been overseeing the house. I think if that's what concerns you, then you should make arrangements to visit. Haley has done a fantastic job in putting life back into that house. The neighbors have grown fond of her and her daughter." He pushed ahead before they could fire more questions at him. "Yes, I'm attracted to her. And we've been spending a lot of time together."

"Is she coming on Saturday?" Sheena pressed, as she gathered the dishes and headed to the kitchen.

"I don't know," Pierce replied.

Chapter 9

Pierce's house nestled in an elegant cul-de-sac with estates that featured grand, beautifully manicured landscapes. His home sat on an elevated lot at the top of the driveway with a double door garage and three expansive levels.

Unlike her home, which had a front porch and country-style architecture, this house had a more modern face. Haley adjusted the overnight bag on her shoulder. She had to take a deep breath to continue walking up the path to the front door.

"Hi. I'm glad you made it," Pierce said as he stood in the open doorway.

Haley looked at him, thinking that he couldn't look any better in a lightweight white cotton shirt and shorts. He offered his hand to invite her in.

Given the mental turmoil that she had undergone on her way to the decision to accept his invite, she was glad that she had decided to come. Now she didn't want his hand, she wanted more.

Haley ran toward him and threw her body into his embrace. She kissed him, holding on to his shoulders to anchor the soaring elation that overcame her.

"It feels so good to have you in my arms," Pierce whispered against her hair.

"The feeling is mutual." She followed him into the cool interior of the house. The raised ceilings, decorated rooms and quality furniture made the house look like a model home.

Pierce kept his arm around her waist. She enjoyed the warmth of his body and the feel of his skin brushing against hers. As she walked through the foyer, past the elegant living room, down the hall into the kitchen, she thought how vast the house seemed for one person. Pierce didn't strike her as the partying type who would have floods of people filling the space.

"Oh, my! How beautiful." Flowers decorated an enclosed porch that had lit votive candles along the sides. The scent of peaches filled the air and the heady, fruity fragrance propelled her farther into the house. "I love the smell of peaches. It makes me feel young." Haley giggled, a little embarrassed to admit something so personal.

"I would do anything for you," Pierce said. He moved in and out of the room, bringing in containers that she recognized as catered dinner entrées.

"I'm learning to accept your strengths," Haley replied. She walked over to inhale the aromas of the food. Beef, chicken and cheese burritos, Spanish rice and black beans were in the numerous containers. Her appetite stirred under the wonderful mixture of meat, sauces and spices. "Let's talk while we eat."

"Not a problem. Your stomach's growl begs to be fed."

She helped herself, then got comfortable on the cushions. The area had been set up for an indoor picnic. Pierce had chosen a perfect setting. There were no climate issues or annoying bugs. An overhead fan circulated the air and made the humidity bearble.

"You are too romantic for your own good," she said as he spread several layers of blankets and tablecloths on the ground. Each piece complemented the peach-and-gold color décor of the room. "Did Laura help you with this?" She leaned over to share a kiss.

"I would lie, but I'm going to have to brag. Laura did send me to this store filled with wicker, linens and these candles. I did a survey among five women. They told me what to do," he confessed.

"You're a very resourceful man. What would you have done without their help?"

"Fixed waffles and told you about the lovefest I have planned."

She laughed.

"The women said that focusing on the food is a good thing, but shouldn't be the defining factor. They told me to focus on ambience." He scooted closer to her and kissed her shoulder.

"I don't want to go to your bedroom. I'm afraid that I may freeze up on you, nerves and all. I like it here."

"Not a problem." He walked over to the wall

and pressed a button. A privacy screen rolled down each window panel.

"I can still see."

"That's the idea. We can see outside and still admire the outdoors. My neighbors, however, will have to return to their prime-time shows for the evening drama."

"Oh darn, and I was hoping to be the cause of gossip in your neighborhood," she teased.

"Not on your life. The citations are too costly, even if it would be worth it," he said and chuckled huskily. He settled beside her and reached for his glass of margarita. She followed suit. "To family, friends and beyond."

"Hear, hear." She sipped at her margarita, enjoying the accurate balance of bitter sweetness and alcohol.

She barely had time to set down her glass when Pierce pulled her across his lap and into his arms. She remained cradled next to his body looking into eyes that overflowed with desire.

She blushed to think that she couldn't hide her naked response from him. Her entire body ached for his touch. She arched against him and offered her mouth, shuddering as his lips brushed hers.

"Don't tease me," she begged.

"We've got all night."

Haley tried to follow his rules, concentrating on restraint. As he planted small kisses down her neck to the opening of her shirt, her desire tested her control like a raging flood seeking freedom. He unbuttoned her shirt, his fingers carelessly brushing against her skin. Zapping her with a stun gun would have had less effect than the strong energy that generated and flowed between them whenever his skin made contact with hers.

He unsnapped her bra and slid the flimsy piece aside. She swore that if he didn't stop playing around her sensitive nipples with his tongue, she would pull out each strand of his hair.

He kissed each peak and she moaned, not caring if she sounded like an animal on the prowl. She pulled open his shirt, sure that she heard a couple buttons hit the floor. She'd think about restitution for the collateral damage later. His chest hair was low, almost nonexistent. She ran her hands over his chest, feeling the muscles twitch and harden under her touch.

They both reached their limit in pretending that haste didn't have a place in their foreplay. Pierce pulled at his pants, sliding them down his hips. Haley finished undressing, handing him a condom. "I figured it was my turn," she said.

On their knees they faced each other, breathing heavily. The glow of the candles threw a romantic, dreamlike quality onto their private cocoon.

Haley clasped hands with Pierce, inching forward until her breasts touched his chest. Then she kissed a path from the indentation at the base of his neck, over his Adam's apple, to his chin. Pierce definitely had physical beauty, but she was drawn to the tender nature of this man in his professional and personal life. His sensitivity was her biggest turn on.

He had beautified his home, not knowing if she would come. That showed how much he wanted her, though he hadn't pressured her. Without any doubt, she knew that she had fallen in love with him. *Was loving this man a good idea?* Haley couldn't contemplate that question right now. In this moment, she was with him. Her heart echoed the sentiment repeatedly as she slid her hands up his chest and around his neck.

Falling for Pierce was like standing on the edge of a beautiful pool. One part of her wanted to test the water with one toe. Her wilder side dictated that she jump in and let her survival mode kick in as she scrambled to the surface.

"I'm ready. On three," she said to Pierce.

"One. Two. Three," Pierce counted, not missing a beat.

Pierce lowered her onto the pillows. She raised her hips to bid him welcome.

Their bodies connected in a rhythm that pulsed with their need and their hunger for each other. Haley surrendered all her inhibitions to ride each sensual wave that coursed through her entire body.

Pierce played with her, teasing a response from between her legs. The mind-blowing pleasure he elicited made her quiver as he delved with masterful strokes. As he increased the tempo, she wrapped the blankets around them, holding him prisoner in her sexual paradise. His grunts mixed with her moans. Their passion raised the temperature on her inside, as well as on her skin.

Their embrace tightened, closing out any space between them. Again, he increased the tempo. Haley bore down, feeling the pressure rise as she floated up and over rolling waves of pleasure, each higher than the last. She licked her lips, wanting to say something, scream, cry, moan as her body answered his call to join in the erotic explosion. They hung on to each other, riding the course until the end.

"Haley, will you spend the night?"

"Only if we have an encore performance."

He kissed her softly. They lay happy and exhausted looking out into the dark backyard. Most of the candles had burned out. They wanted to stay close until the last candle winked out, leaving them in the darkness to fall asleep.

Pierce awoke on Saturday, hoping that the night before wasn't a dream. And if it wasn't a dream, he hoped that Haley was still beside him. He turned over to see her curled up with the covers tucked under her chin, her hair splayed against the pillow.

One look at her sleeping form and his appetite stirred like a sleeping giant. He played with her hair, following its gentle curl that lay along her cheek. She moved slightly when his finger touched her skin. He thought of himself as the luckiest man.

"You may not know it, but you've got my heart, Haley Sanders," he whispered. One day, he hoped to have the courage to tell her. For now, he'd settle for her subconscious.

He kissed her cheek and then the corner of her lips, before engulfing her mouth with his. She stirred under his attention, coming awake in a sleepy haze. He saw her immediate reaction as she tried to get her bearings.

"Good morning, sleepyhead," he said.

She pulled up the cover and looked beneath. "Oh."

"We're in the buff," he confirmed.

"There's no one else in this house, correct?"

"That's right." He rolled away and got out of bed. "How about a glass of orange juice?"

She nodded, but not before he caught her admiring his naked body.

"You can have your way with me when I return," he joked.

"Good. I'd hate to think that Friday night was all you had in you."

"Be right back." He grinned and headed for the kitchen. Suddenly he wished that he hadn't invited his family and Morton for the Saturday afternoon get-together. He'd much rather make love to Haley all day until Laura returned with Beth.

"Here's your beverage." He handed her the glass and then scooted under the covers to play. "I've got to tell you something," he said.

"What?" She sipped at her juice while playfully slapping his fingers away from her nipples.

"My family and some friends are coming over for a cookout this afternoon." He caressed her shoulder, planning his next move. He planned to conquer her inch by inch.

"That scares me," Haley said.

"Don't worry. I'll be there."

"See, now that worries me. The fact that you have to be here with me makes me think that your family has sharp, big fangs that may gobble me up."

"You've met Laura," he said.

"Yeah, but somehow, I get the feeling that your other sister isn't quite like Laura."

He knew this should be a serious discussion, but when the covers fell to her waist, all thought of family scuttled out of his brain.

Now wasn't a time for talking. He pulled her on top of him and kissed her with pent-up passion that had lingered from the night. Luckily, there were no clothes to slide off bodies and discard. Haley straddled him in her undressed state. His body woke up as his mind registered the various parts of her anatomy. He slipped on his protection.

She worked her hips, riding him, taking him to

the point of screaming. Her hips gyrating above his sent him into a frenzy, devoid of any coherent speech. Her tempo, so unlike his, teased and soothed so that she toyed with him in a delightfully unfair manner.

Alone in their world, he surrendered to her. She was his queen. As such, he waited for her to reach her peak. That moment when the moans started down deep in her body and he could feel it through her hips. Not until she came with a climactic force did he follow suit.

Pierce didn't have much time to prepare for his cookout. Thankfully, he had purchased everything he needed the day before. All he had to do was get the grill heated and ready for use. He was sure that Morton would come with a big appetite.

"Pierce, someone is coming up the driveway." Haley sat in the living room, peering out a curtained window.

"That's Omar." Pierce opened the door, making sure that he didn't burden Haley with that task.

"Hey, big brother," Omar said as Pierce closed the door behind him.

"Let me introduce you." Pierce made the introductions, keeping an eye on Omar, who had a knack for blurting out things that were better left unsaid. "By the way, where is Sheena?" Pierce asked.

"She couldn't make it," Omar replied. Pierce looked at Omar for more of an explanation. "I don't have a clue what came up," the younger man said.

"That's fine. Morton will be here soon," Pierce said and tried to hide the disappointment. He hoped that Sheena wasn't trying to make a statement by being a no-show.

The doorbell rang. Pierce opened the door. "Welcome," Pierce said. Morton stood in his doorway, looking cavalier and chic. Omar and Morton spent the next few minutes exchanging handshakes.

"We'll be in the kitchen when you're done playing hand jive." Pierce took Haley's hand and walked into the kitchen. "Think that I may have to take you up on your offer of help after all."

"Good. I'd hate to be sitting off to the side simply watching all the fun," she said.

For the next few hours, Pierce entertained his brother, mentor and girlfriend. Laura and Beth were off on a shopping trip and he did miss Sheena not being there. The assembled company had a congenial atmosphere that allowed for them to have a wonderful cookout. Several times he looked over to Haley and couldn't be more pleased when she'd wink back or respond with a big, happy smile. He finally relaxed and enjoyed his company when Morton whispered, "You did good," as he walked over to fill his plate with cake and ice cream.

Haley looked out her office window for the umpteenth time, unable to concentrate. The report she was working on was due the next morning and she'd have to pull an all-nighter to finish it. That meant having to call Laura to keep an eye on Beth for the evening.

Beth wouldn't be happy. She remembered that she'd promised to take Beth to buy new tennis shoes that evening. They would have to postpone that task until the weekend.

"Haley, how's the report coming? Do you have a draft for me to preview?" Her boss, Mr. Jackson, had startled her with his unannounced appearance at her office door.

Haley jumped and hit the button to get rid of the screensaver of her daughter's smiling face. "I broke it into two parts." She punched the print key, a bit nervous that her rough draft would be viewed by her new boss. "The first part explains why we need to move cautiously with any development plans for the city."

"What?" He walked over to the printer and pulled out the paper before the entire document printed. "We discussed this. I told you that we were not going to get into anything political. This is the city council. There are people on it ready to pounce on an opening like this." He waved the partial report over his head and slammed it down on the desk in front of her. "Didn't you understand my instructions? Why do you give me so much grief?" Jackson glared at her and then fixed his suit, his eyes never leaving her face.

Haley didn't back down, returning her boss's stare. Apparently her boss seemed to like these showdowns, as if they were two gunfighters sizing each other up before the shootout. Frankly, Haley found them exhausting. Had Strayer had to put up with this? Maybe it was a man thing. Jackson never held a grudge afterward, treating their confrontations as differences of opinion.

With her re-emerging self-confidence and struggling to stay steady, Haley looked at Jackson and saw a partial image of her husband. The main differences between the two men were superficial. The two were very alike.

Jackson could sputter all he wanted. As she read pieces of the material and data, she felt confident that she hadn't miscommunicated anything. "Mr. Jackson, I think you should read the entire report. You'll see that I'm recommending the city council take a more prominent role in any redevelopment plans."

"I want to see the rest of it as soon as you're finished."

Haley shook her head and sighed. Jackson reminded her of a volcano. He erupted, emitted steam, settled down and then went back into a dormant phase. And yet there was a sting to his criticisms that she had come to expect and accept. He always apologized when she could prove her point. She'd accept that as some weird sign of respect.

Having a higher profile job increased the exposure to Jackson and his boss. Moments like this made her wish that her previous boss was still around. He'd provided a buffer between her and upper management. Thank goodness for her staff; they had worked hard to prove that their department had the talent for success. She was very proud of them. This pride and responsibility to protect were her armor when she faced Jackson.

She worked through the morning, using coffee as her only reason for quick breaks. Caffeine made her nerves a jittery mess. On edge, she finished typing the report with clammy fingers.

Her phone rang. She debated whether to answer it. A glance at the clock showed that Beth was in her last class for the day. Maybe the babysitter was calling because she couldn't pick up Beth.

The receptionist's voice played over the intercom. "Haley, you have a call."

Haley acknowledged the message, thanking the young woman. Once the transfer was made, she prompted, "Hello."

"Glad to hear that you're still in Hampton Mews. When my lawyer said that you hadn't called back, I attributed your lack of a response to your picking another remote spot in Maryland as a hiding place."

"What do you want, Vernon?" As if she didn't know. She'd responded to his letter with a curt note stating that she had no intention of reconciling with him.

"I missed you."

"No one to host your parties?"

"Since when did you get bitter?" He said it softly. Haley knew instantly that he was angry. He hated when she was flip or sarcastic. "I want my family to be together. We are a unit," he said.

"I've got all the family that I need," she countered. He'd never been a husband or father, but more a dictator with genuine fondness for his daughter.

"You don't sound yourself," Vernon said.

"You mean the timid mouse that you held in contempt."

"I'm not going to argue with you while you're in this mental state. How is Beth? I want to see her," he said.

Haley took a deep breath, well, several deep breaths. He always mentioned her mental state when he no longer wanted to discuss matters with her. How could she have ever thought that she loved this man? Her youth had been a contributing factor. Beth was a product of that honeymoon period filled with starry-eyed naiveté.

As Haley's marriage had turned sour, she'd kept her heartache to herself. She didn't believe in discussing grown-up issues with her daughter.

And she refused to paint Beth's father in a bad light. But that didn't mean that she was about to roll over and forgive the past just because Vernon demanded to see Beth.

"If you recall, the judge made the visitation and custody decisions about Beth." Haley stared out the window, wondering how her day had taken such a nosedive into muck so quickly.

"I've taken counseling and anger-management classes. I have even redecorated a room for Beth and checked into the best schools. I think the judge will be willing to give me a second chance. And I'm willing to give you a second chance. Perhaps we can fall in love again."

His lawyer must have made headway with the court for another hearing. The thought sent shivers down her spine. The judge hadn't wanted to give her full custody the first time. If Vernon showed on paper that he was a changed man, then the judge could overturn his previous decision.

She wanted Beth to have contact with her father, but she didn't want Vernon to use their relationship for selfish purposes. The thought of his manipulations ignited her anger to full blast. But she had to be very careful.

"Vernon, as I've said, I'm not interested in

moving from here. I know that you want to see Beth more often, and I'm willing to work with you," she explained.

"Of course, it doesn't have to be my way or your way. I can compromise. I'd like to make a few visits, then we can play it by ear."

"Okay," Haley said quietly. Even to her ears, she sounded unsure.

"How about this weekend?"

"Fine." But it wasn't fine. Things were moving too quickly. She had to think. She wanted to talk to Beth. Vernon wasn't giving her any time to adjust, bulldozing as he usually did to keep her off-kilter. "I think Beth would like to see you," she finished, her mind no where near the project that she'd been working on for Jackson.

"I'll come get her."

"No!" Haley fired back with alarm. "I'll bring her to you." She didn't want Vernon in the same town, or anywhere near her home. He may have steamrolled his way so far, but she wasn't budging on that point.

"Fine," he said.

They finished up the conversation with the details and logistics for dropping off Beth and picking her up that Sunday.

After the call with Vernon, Haley turned to finish her project. Her mind was more troubled than ever.

Haley honked the horn. She had taken the afternoon off to meet Beth immediately after school to get on the road for her trip to their old neighborhood. Friday could go down as a personal low from the time that she'd awoken that morning. Haley's mind had constantly wandered throughout the day.

She honked the horn again and stuck her head out the window. "Beth!"

Haley waited for her daughter to come running out of the house with her overnight bag. After a few seconds, she turned off the engine, muttering under her breath. Given their late start, they'd be traveling through the rush hour and darkness, Haley thought glumly. Just then Laura appeared on the porch.

Haley was used to seeing Laura at her house, but she didn't usually come this early. She tried not to think that perhaps something was wrong.

"Beth is around back helping Pierce," Laura said.

"Helping Pierce?" Haley walked along the side

of the house, listening for any sounds that could give her a hint of what Pierce and Beth might be working on.

She rounded the house and almost bumped into a ladder propped against its back side. Laura walked up beside her. Both women stared up at the roof. Haley cupped her mouth to hold back her scream.

"Hey, Mom, I'm helping to fix a gutter. Pierce said the last rain soaked the side of the house and may have seeped into the first floor." Beth looked down at them from her perch on the roof. She leaned forward and waved.

"Beth, would you come down please," Haley said. She used a soft, cajoling tone that she was far from feeling. Heights didn't bother her daughter, but the visual sure did a number on *her* nerves. "Where the heck is Pierce?"

"He was here a few minutes, ago," Beth said.

Pierce walked into the backyard, his forehead wrinkled, looking perplexed. Haley folded her arms, waiting for him to look at her or at least to look at Beth.

"Why would you let Beth go on the roof?" Haley asked.

Pierce finally caught sight of her. His ready

smile instantly vanished as he ran forward to where she stood.

"Beth, didn't I tell you to wait?" Pierce dumped the materials he had in his hands into Haley's arms. He took a step toward the ladder. "Wait right there. For heaven's sake, sit down, you're making me nervous," he said.

Beth stepped toward the ladder, still grinning. "I can do it. Watch me." She turned and eased one foot down onto the first rung. Then she swung her other foot around and reached for the second rung.

"I'm coming. Don't move another inch," Pierce shouted.

Haley watched the scene unfold. Once Beth's feet touched solid ground, she was going to wring her neck.

"It'll be okay, Haley." Laura had placed an arm around her shoulder. "Pierce will get her down safely." Haley was grateful for Laura's attempt to calm her nerves, but she felt Laura's fingers digging into her shoulder as Beth eased down a few more rungs.

Haley closed her eyes as relief coursed through her body. She heard a sound that she knew came from the ladder. She opened her eyes to see Beth dangling with one hand. Her screams tore through the air.

Her daughter had lost her footing.

"Pierce, save her!" Haley clutched Laura's hand.

"Hang on," Pierce ordered. He moved quickly up the ladder inches away from Beth.

"I can't." Beth's hand slipped. She fell through the air. Pierce's hand barely missed her as he reached for any part of her body as she passed him.

Haley didn't know if she was screaming or crying. She knelt beside her daughter, moaning her name.

"I'll call an ambulance," Laura said and dashed off toward the house.

Beth didn't respond. Her eyes were closed and she lay very still.

"Pierce, help my little girl." She grabbed his sleeve until he lowered himself next to Beth. "Make her wake up, please."

Chapter 10

Haley loosened the dirt with her fingers. She wished that Beth would join her. Haley was convinced that her daughter was missing out on a wonderful experience. Instead Beth remained in the house, in her room. Her arm was still in a cast, but the nasty bruise on her forehead had faded. Maybe she ought to be glad that her daughter was reading, although her book selection appeared to be focused on one subject—dieting.

"Care for some help?"

"Where did you come from?" Haley initially

jumped at Pierce's voice, but now her pulse raced for a different reason.

"Checking on my property. Making sure that there are no wild parties, surprise tenants not on the lease, you know, the regular stuff a landlord has to do."

"I'm burying the beer cans as we speak," Haley said and wrinkled her nose.

"I'll let you off with a warning, this time." He knelt next to her.

She felt him watching her, studying her process of digging shallow holes, gingerly placing the young plants in the holes and refilling each hole. With a final pat, she sat up on the special wheeled gardening stool.

"Looks easy enough," Pierce said.

"Good. You can start over there and then we'll meet in the middle." She'd already suspected that she'd be finished with her side before he finished his. At least there was one thing that she had mastery of over the small-town doctor.

They worked in easy silence. Haley had remembered to wear a hat with a wide enough brim that covered the upper part of her face and the back of her neck. Pierce wasn't quite so fortunate.

"Let's take a break," she said, thinking gardening was tougher than it looked.

"I have six more plants for this row," Pierce said. He stabbed into the dirt with the small spade she'd given him and flung it aside.

"Keep doing that and you won't have enough soil to refill the hole. Be gentle." She scooted herself over to him. "Here, let me show you." She took the little gardening spade from him.

Many manicurists had scolded her for the state of her hands. They'd listen in horror as she told them that she didn't wear gloves when gardening. Once upon a time, she'd been fastidious about such things.

Gardening had proved to be one of those activities that she couldn't enjoy unless her hands touched the soil. There was something magical and powerful that connected her to all living things when she ran her fingers through the dirt. The little plants allowed her to admire and create beauty. In the garden, she didn't have to live up to anyone's ideals.

"You have a knack for this," Pierce complimented. "I bet you had a banging backyard at your previous house."

"I guess I did." They'd had a landscape

company that had mowed, trimmed hedges and performed cosmetic touches to their expansive four-acre property. But she'd had a small plot that they hadn't been allowed to touch. It had been her little playground with garden vegetables and flowers. Vernon had hated the garden and hated seeing her working in it.

"What else are you doing?" Pierce asked after they'd completed the row.

"I think that's it."

"We don't get to admire our handiwork? Well, mostly your efforts," Pierce said.

"I'll give you points for trying." She smiled at him.

He returned the honor with a smile. Haley felt as if a sunlamp had been directed onto her face. A smile shouldn't have that kind of hypnotic effect. His eyes were magical, too. His gaze had the ability to surround her with an intensity that featured honesty. Its hypnotic effect could only be due to Pierce's straight-shooter character.

"Looks like you have a few war wounds." She brushed her hands off on her shorts and then stretched out his arm for her further examination.

"Minor," he said, yet he didn't take his arm away.

"I've got a medicine cabinet filled with all sorts of remedies. You tend to do that when you have a kid."

Haley blushed under his stare. Maybe she was talking too much, but she couldn't help it. He made her so nervous.

She turned to head toward the house. He followed. His arm that she had held moments ago had slipped around her waist. She looked up in his face for an answer. All she could do was blink.

He was always the gentleman around her. And those eyes at this minute didn't erase that impression. His demeanor had been overlaid by his attraction to her.

"Here, let me get that," he said. He adjusted the spaghetti strap that had fallen from her shoulder to her arm.

"Thanks." *Thank you for being attentive. Thank you, my gorgeous landord, who can rev my heart into high gear. Thank you for touching my skin,* she thought. She was surprised that touching her hadn't scorched his finger. *And especially thank you for not removing your hand that is cupping my shoulder, where I can feel each finger leave an imprint,* she concluded.

She tiptoed. Seemed like a good idea since he

was at least half a foot or more taller. His eyes narrowed, but he remained silent. Nothing in his body language stopped her or made her hesitate.

Before the outside world seeped into her consciousness, she slid her hand up his neck and pulled his head down to her.

She'd wanted to taste his lips from the first day when she'd come upon him in the old shed. At the time, she had filed it under being a lonely, divorced woman.

Her lips parted, waiting for the experience that she craved. She was only vaguely aware of his other hand pulling her into an embrace that pulled her body against his.

Her tongue slipped between his lips and she let her imagination run wild. She kissed him, enjoying the idea that maybe she'd shocked him. His surprise did stop him from responding to her. Though she had limited experience with men, she deemed him an excellent kisser. She peeked through one eye to see if he did it with his eyes closed.

At her slight pause, Pierce sensed Haley's examination of him. He took it as his cue to lead this dance. Not that he needed any encouragement.

The feel of Haley in his arms awakened a

hunger within that was new, vibrant and addictive. He hungrily plunged his tongue into the sweetness of her mouth. A groan eased out of him like a lazy note. She answered with a soft moan that made him hold her tighter.

"Well, isn't this a cozy picture."

Pierce pulled away from Haley, recognizing the husky accuser. He tried to keep an arm around Haley, but she had stepped back out of his reach. Two options were ahead of him. He could tend to Haley and reassure her or he could tend to his sister who glared at him.

He introduced Haley to his sister, noting Sheena's open hostility.

"I came by to see who was renting my mother's house," Sheena stated.

"It's me and my daughter, Beth," Haley offered.

Pierce remained silent, hoping that Sheena would be on her way. But Sheena resumed her seat on the back steps and proceeded to eat an apple. Damn. If she wanted to air the family disagreement over selling the house in front of Haley, he couldn't do much to stop her.

"Miss, what's your name?" Sheena asked.

"You may call me Haley."

"You're planning to buy this house?"

Haley nodded.

"Are you planning to play house, too?"

"That's enough, Sheena. Haley, could you give us a second?" Pierce said.

"No problem." Haley had locked stares with Sheena. She walked past his sister, never looking at him. He waited until the back door clicked shut.

"Walk with me," Pierce said to Sheena.

Sheena didn't budge.

"Please."

She smiled, but her expression looked more like a snarl.

He led the way to the bench that had been cleaned and repainted. He didn't take a seat until she sat.

"What was that all about?" he asked.

"I could say the same about you. I know that you like to help the damsel in distress. But it looks to me as if she may have ulterior motives," Sheena said.

"You don't know anything about her," he replied.

"And whose fault would that be?"

"I would have included you, Sheena. But

sometimes you are so impulsive, like a few minutes ago."

"A few minutes ago, I was protecting my assets, unlike you."

"Haley isn't a money-grubbing character."

"Nope, just another woman who needs a father for her child and a rich husband. Guess you answered the ad," she said derisively.

"Don't jump ahead. I'm simply enjoying Haley's company."

Sheena sighed. "I can't stay mad at you, Pierce. We've been through the heavy drama, but we've had some great times."

"Does this mean that I can come for Sunday dinner?" He grinned. Sheena's lift of his exile did lighten his mood.

Sheena gave him a brief hug. "Feel free to bring your new friend and her daughter."

"I'm not sure about that."

"I promise to behave. But if my brother is going to act like a love-starved man, no matter how true the label, then I need to keep close tabs on the subject at hand."

"Give her a break. She's had a rough time of it."

"First you fall under her spell of seduction. Now you're all up in her business and playing the spokesperson. Boy, are you falling hard?" She laughed, patting him on his shoulder before leaving the yard.

Pierce watched her get into her car. A smug expression remained on her face. He suspected that he would be the subject of discussion and jokes to her husband.

Plus he couldn't deny that he was happy to be back in the fold. Since the house was proving to be such a divisive factor in the family, maybe once they met Haley, his siblings would feel more comfortable about the sale of the house.

He looked toward the back of the house. The moment had been lost.

Haley didn't move from her vantage point that allowed her to see the animated conversation between Pierce and his sister. The hug at the end had to mean something, since his sister wore a smile that hadn't been there at her initial meeting.

Now Pierce was coming inside the house.

His sister's visit saved her from making a further fool of herself. If he thought that she was going to fall into his arms again, he was mistaken. But just to be sure, she sat at the small table in the kitchen.

"Sorry about my sister bursting in," he said.

"Seems like she was concerned about the house. And I think she was a little concerned for you," Haley said.

"Sheena is a bit protective," he said.

"Sounds a tad territorial, too." Haley remembered the woman's highly critical survey.

"Only at first. I explained your situation to her and now she wants to invite you to a cookout at her place."

"What could you have said that would bring on such an invite?"

"It's for you and Beth," Pierce added.

"I would consider going, if you told me why your sister changed her mind."

He raised her chin with the crook of his finger. Softly he stroked her lip with his thumb before placing a kiss on her mouth. "She wanted to meet my girlfriend."

"Girlfriend?"

"Welcome, Haley," Sheena said and shook her hand. Haley returned the greeting, exchanging small talk.

Beth stood at her side, still pouting from an earlier disagreement. She hadn't wanted to come to the cookout. Beth would've preferred to spend the afternoon in her room.

Haley didn't like how much time Beth wanted to spend away from her. She knew that teens wanted independence, but Beth's desire to be alone didn't strike her as a need for independence. Rather it seemed more a sign of anger.

"I'm glad you made it." Pierce escorted her to the deck. "Hey, Beth, Sheena's got the latest video-game system downstairs, if you want to check it out with the other kids."

Beth shrugged, but it didn't stop her from acting on his invitation and taking off toward the basement.

"You worry too much about her," he said.

"Can't help it. I don't think that she's adjusting as fast as I thought she would. I picked this town, this community, even the house because I thought the change would do her good," Haley said. "It doesn't seem to be working out."

"She's having normal growing pains. Be patient with her."

Haley nodded, not feeling as confident as Pierce sounded.

"It'll be okay," Pierce reassured. "Let's grab a hot dog. Looks like they just came off the grill."

"Sounds delicious. I want mine with lots of ketchup and mustard."

"Onions and pickles?" Pierce said.

Haley wrinkled her nose. "No kissing then," she whispered.

Pierce pulled her to him and planted a wet, sloppy kiss on her mouth before pulling away and leaving her with a huge grin. "Figured that I'd get started before I feasted on the onions," he said.

"Looks like my timing is always off." Sheena looked at them. At least this time she was smiling, Haley thought. It appeared Sheena's suspicion was gone, and had been replaced with open friendship.

"I'll go get the hot dogs." Pierce squeezed her shoulder. He probably sensed her panic that he was leaving her side.

"Let's grab a couple of chairs in the shade," Sheena offered, gesturing to the chairs.

Once they were seated, Haley waited for Sheena to begin the conversation.

"How do you like our city?"

"It's beautiful. Seems like a growing city. I see a lot of houses being built," Haley said.

"It's a city that's taking the overflow from

Frederick and Baltimore. Many people can't afford to live in those cities. I only hope that it doesn't get too overpopulated. Then we'll have problems like crime, overcrowded schools and traffic jams."

"Sorry to be contributing to the demise of your country living." Haley wanted to keep quiet, but she felt Sheena's contempt for the newcomers to the city expand to include her. She wasn't going to let her get away with it, even if she was Pierce's sister.

"It's not an accusation, simply a fact," Sheena said. "How do you like the house?"

"I love it," Haley replied.

"That's where we grew up."

"And no one wanted it?"

"We all went our separate ways. After my mother died, we rented it, but the occupants were never ideal. Several of them had kids who ruined the walls," Sheena said. "The house has been empty for a year now."

"Well, that won't be a problem with me and my daughter. Plus we're planning to buy the place and make it our home."

"Pierce may not have told you, but not all of us are in agreement with this sale."

"Is that why you're taking your anger out on me?"

Sheena pulled back, clearly shocked that Haley had taken the offensive.

"I understand your attachment to your family home, but I need a stable environment for my daughter. Beth is going through a difficult time right now."

"Where's her father?"

"I'm divorced," Haley said.

"And you think you can handle work, home and everything else that comes along with being a single parent?"

"Are you a single parent?"

Sheena shook her head.

"That may explain why you're talking to me with no respect," Haley said.

Haley needed the house. The price suited her. The financing worked to her advantage. Pierce was an added bonus, but she wasn't going to take this woman's crap to get all those things.

Nevertheless, she kept a close eye on Sheena's reaction. Her shock had dissipated, but Sheena's face had hardened into a no-nonsense expression.

"I'm hard-pressed to show respect when I find

the tenant throwing down with the landlord after a month," Sheena said.

If this was a fight, Haley would accuse Sheena of dealing a low blow. And it hurt as bad as if it had really happened. She couldn't get indignant because of Sheena's honesty.

One month and she'd acted without restraint. Pierce looked damned good, but so did other men and she didn't end in a lip-lock with them.

He'd be on somebody's list as an eligible bachelor, especially with his being a doctor. Yet, Haley had been married to a corporate executive and knew from firsthand knowledge that credentials didn't make a man.

No, Pierce meant more to her than just a meal ticket. He lit up her life every time she spent time with him. He genuinely listened to her, offering insights rather than making demands of her.

"Thank you for inviting me. It's time for me to leave," Haley said and stood, wishing that she and Sheena could have gotten off to a better start.

She didn't wait for Sheena to insult her further. She went in search of her daughter. When she found Beth, they would leave. If she saw Pierce, she would explain why she was leaving, but if not, his sister could give him whatever explanation suited her.

The raised voices of children having fun spilled out of the basement as Haley approached the door. She hoped Beth wouldn't resist her. This was not the time or place for a scene.

Despite the volume, there were only a handful of kids down there. Beth sat in front of a large TV with game remotes, playing against another kid. Haley positioned herself to see what was going on without distracting Beth. Her daughter was in the lead and had a few boisterous cheerleaders on her side.

A familiar deep voice urged Beth to be careful as she rappelled off a cliff, shooting at planes overhead.

"I was wondering where you got to." Pierce moved out of the shadows to stand next to Haley. He slid an arm around her waist. She loved the feel of his body next to hers.

"Sheena had me on lockdown."

"All this time?"

Haley nodded. "It wasn't a pretty sight." She wished that she didn't have to say anything, but he had to know why she was leaving. "I'm getting Beth so that we can leave," Haley told Pierce.

He pushed off from the wall and stood directly in front of her. His tall frame blocked Beth's performance from Haley's view as the other children cheered. She could hear high fives go around the room.

"Are you leaving because of Sheena?"

She didn't answer. It didn't matter. Maybe Sheena was a blessing in disguise because Haley had been forced to deal with the fact that she was being silly and young at heart over Pierce.

"I'll be right back. Please stay until I return." She didn't answer. "Haley, don't leave without me."

"Pierce, as much as I would like for you to take up the fight for me, it's not necessary. I'm leaving because I'm tired. Beth has had a long day. She has her doctor's appointment in the morning."

"I'll help you with Beth. Give me a call when you get home."

Half an hour later, Haley drove from Sheena's home.

"I had a good time, Mom," Beth said.

"I'm glad to hear. Did you get a chance to eat?"

"Yep."

Haley looked at her daughter. She was glad to see a smile on her face. Although she was still as thin as a rail, it sounded as if they had rounded an important bend in their relationship.

"Where's Pierce? I'm surprised he didn't come with us."

"He's talking to his sister." Haley looked over to Beth. "You don't mind him coming over?"

Beth looked at her. "I know that he makes you happy. And when he's around, you don't bother me as much."

Haley was left openmouthed, staring at her daughter. Then she dissolved in laughter. She guessed her daughter had a point.

"I'm really glad you don't mind," Haley said. She took Beth's hand and rubbed it against her cheek.

"Whatever makes you happy. He doesn't make you cry."

"You knew," Haley blurted. "I tried to hide it."

"I know you tried to make my life run smoothly, but there's no point in hiding the ugliness," Beth said.

Haley turned onto her street, amazed at the adult-toned conversation that she was having with Beth. She had to constantly look over at her to determine whether her daughter was serious.

"Stop growing up so fast on me." Haley grinned at her, and was amazed when her daughter grinned back at her.

When they entered the house, Haley heard the phone ring. She hurried to answer it.

"Hey, I'm outside," Pierce said.

"Meet you on the back steps."

She hung up the phone. A small measure of fear made her hesitate. What if his sister had turned him against her?

She paused at the door, resting her forehead against it. She could handle any bad news.

"Invite him in, Mom. You're like a high-school couple sitting on the steps talking. I'm going to bed now. No need to worry about me," Beth said behind her.

Haley figured that there was no use pretending she didn't care for Pierce for Beth's sake. She opened the door to invite Pierce into the house.

In the doorway stood Pierce *and* his sister.

"Dr. Masterson."

Pierce looked up from the patient's file. "Yes, Dr. Peters."

"Is everything okay? You're a little quiet today. No bad jokes. No sugar-free lollipops. Do we need to switch places?"

Pierce grinned. He set down his pen. "Dr. Peters, the day that you get me to sit on your couch and spill all my dark secrets is the day that I move out of town."

"That's what everyone says. But you'd be surprised how good you'll feel after talking things out," Dr. Peters said.

Pierce resumed writing notes in the file. Mr. Peters had been his first patient when he'd moved back into town and started his practice. Dr. Peters was a well-known psychologist and professor at the nearby university with prestigious awards and writing credits.

"Seriously, though, can I help you?" Dr. Peters asked.

"It's a woman." Pierce snapped the file shut. "You can button your shirt. You're all set."

"I've made lots of money listening to men pour their hearts out about their women."

"That sarcastic tone does nothing to make me want to tell you anything," Pierce said.

"It's not sarcasm." Dr. Peters squirmed his way off the table. Pierce went through the usual motions of offering assistance, knowing that his hand would be brushed aside.

"Men want a straightforward answer as to how to deal with women. Don't spend your money figuring them out, spend money figuring out yourself. Then you'll understand where your better half is coming from."

"Hmm. Sounds like sound advice. Since I

know myself and I don't have any issues, then I'm fine."

"Spoken like a true male." Dr. Peters extended his hand. Pierce shook it. "Well, Doc, guess the old ticker still has a few more beats," Dr. Peters said. Pierce nodded. "Good. Then I'm heading to the mountains to do some rock climbing this weekend."

"Don't forget to wear a helmet."

Dr. Peters opened the door, then paused.

"Yes," Pierce prompted.

"You're so good at looking after others, telling them what they need to do, diagnosing and solving problems. Who does that for you?"

"I do that, Dr. Peters," Pierce answered confidently.

"Wow. Well, I'm heading to the mountains. You're already at the top of yours." He waved and walked down the hall.

"What the heck is that supposed to mean?" Pierce stared after the older man. He had a busy day ahead of him. No time to ponder cryptic messages.

Anyway, he was meeting Haley for lunch. It would have to be a quick one since he had scheduled appointments with a couple of his chattier patients that afternoon. They tended to back up his entire schedule. His peers told him to adopt their fifteen-minute rule, but he wasn't going to do that. If a patient needed extra time, then so be it.

"Dr. Masterson, you have a call on line one."

"Thank you." He depressed the intercom button. He hoped the call wasn't from Haley to cancel their date. "Dr. Masterson, here."

"Hi, it's Beth."

"Oh, this is a pleasant surprise." He frowned, wondering why she sounded so excited.

"I couldn't get hold of Mom. I wanted to let you know that I won't be there this afternoon."

"That's fine." The wall had long been completed. Recently, he had put her to work filing. Haley's main goal was to keep Beth too busy to spend time hanging out with wild friends.

"My dad is here," Beth said.

"Your dad?" Pierce stared at the phone. His throat had gone dry. "Good. I'm glad that your dad is there. With you? In the house?" He only had Haley's accounts of the divorce. Haley's ex didn't seem to be a nice guy. Yet, Beth seemed gleeful that her father was there. "Did you call your mom?"

"I told you. She wasn't at work," Beth said.

Pierce heard a man ask a question in the background. It was too muffled to hear, but he did make out Beth's response. "It's mom's friend. Yes, Daddy, boyfriend," Beth said, adding, "Pierce, I've gotta go. See you later."

The line went dead. He tried Haley's office and her cell phone. There was no answer, so he left messages. He didn't want her going home without him.

Pierce worked through his next two patients. Mrs. Keyes always wanted to fix him up with one of her choir members. Not that he discriminated against age, but he did have his limit. Meanwhile, Mr. Jefferson refused to drink the daily fiber nutrient that Pierce had described. Inevitably, he ended up in Pierce's examination room looking for on-the-spot treatment.

His office was always closed during the lunch break. He didn't have to worry about anyone being left behind when he went to lunch or anyone arriving too early. Most times, he ate lunch in the office. But since he had started seeing Haley, he'd jumped on the opportunity to see her more than once in the day.

In the middle of the business district, there was a deli shop noted for their thick milk shakes. He pulled up in the parking lot, scanning the cars for Haley's. He glanced at his watch. He was five minutes early. If she had gotten Beth's message, she might have gone home.

The little diner buzzed with the lunch crowd. He had to wait for a couple to finish and remove their trash before he nabbed a table. He apologized for hovering over them.

As the lunch hour continued, larger crowds poured into the tiny shop. Many patrons chose carryout. Only the lucky early birds were able to get a table.

Today he would try the chicken chili and garlic toast. Haley would probably have a salad. Occasionally she'd try a bowl of soup.

"Haley, over here." It took her a few seconds to see him waving madly at her. Her face lit up when their eyes met. Immediately his mood lightened and he didn't care that he had a full afternoon ahead of him.

"Were you waiting long?" She pecked him on his cheek.

He shook his head and kissed her on the lips. She giggled and pushed him away.

"I don't know why you're embarrassed to be seen with me?" he questioned petulantly.

"You know darn well that it's because you kiss me and keep kissing me. It took a week to get people from my job to stop teasing me the last time."

"They're just jealous," he said.

She laughed. "Probably. So tell me about your day."

"Let's order and then we can talk." He didn't want to break the news about Beth to her just yet. Her eyes shone with such lightheartedness and easy amusement that he hated to upset her.

She ordered while he held the table. Five minutes later they had their meals in front of them.

"You never said, how was your day?" Haley prompted again.

"Busy, as usual." His soup smelled good, but he hadn't taken a bite yet. "I had a call from Beth. She can't make it this afternoon."

"Oh." Haley frowned. "It's been so busy and I had to go to a couple meetings." She pulled out her cell phone and turned it on. The message light popped on, it's red color announcing that she had voice mail. "Maybe this is Beth. Maybe she told me why she can't make it. I hope you didn't let her pull a fast one on you."

He stayed her hand. At least she had made a dent in her salad. Once he told her the news, he suspected that lunch would be over.

"Beth told me why she wouldn't make it."

Haley put down her fork. He knew there was no way to make this easy for her. "Your husband, I mean ex-husband, is here."

"Here. In town?"

He nodded. "At your house."

She grabbed her pocketbook and pushed back the chair. "You didn't think that was important enough to tell me right away," she accused.

"I left a message." He pushed back his chair and rose. "Damn." He picked up their lunch bills and headed for the cashier.

Haley walked ahead of him. She hadn't said anything further. He impatiently waited for the woman to ring them up. "Haley, would you wait for a minute." He relaxed only a little when she stood outside the diner with her arms folded.

Shoving his change into his pocket, he ran up next to her. "Are you heading over there now?"

"Of course. I didn't know he was coming. I can't believe Beth let him in. I can't believe that he just showed up. I didn't tell him where I lived, not that he couldn't find me. But it's been months since I left and he didn't come to see Beth when she was in the hospital. So what does he want?"

"Honey, take a deep breath. I think that Beth probably contacted him. He's her father and she loves him. Maybe she doesn't understand why you won't see him," he said.

"Darn it. I have a meeting that I have to attend in fifteen minutes. I can't get over there for another two hours."

"I'll go check on Beth," Pierce said.

She looked up at him. "No, I don't think that's a good idea."

"I can be civil," he assured her.

"It's not you I'm worried about."

He grabbed her by the shoulders. "Hey, trust me. I will simply go to the house. Tell Beth that I'm checking on the rail on the porch. It needs tightening anyway."

"You have patients."

"I'll head over to your place now and make sure everything is okay. Then I'll only be about fifteen minutes off my schedule," he said.

"Well, okay," Haley said and smoothed the hair along his sideburn. "You are such a lifesaver."

"I'll call you after I leave the house."

They parted ways so that Haley could get to her

appointment on time. Pierce drove to her house. He had to admit that he was nervous. Was her ex-husband a hulking beast of a man? Would he be a menacing clean-shaven sociopath? Good grief, he couldn't remember the man's name.

He pulled up in front of the house, noting the new red convertible that was parked in the driveway. Normally he would have jumped out the car and raced up the lawn, but now his feet moved like lead, one step at a time. He headed up the three steps onto the front porch and knocked on the door.

It swung open instantly. Beth beamed at him from just inside the door. "Hey, Pierce, come in." Then she looked over her shoulder. "Dad!"

Pierce looked in the direction that Beth had bellowed. He heard the heavy footsteps against the wooden floor. Then he shifted his scrutiny to Beth. She looked fine, positively radiant.

At that moment, the man who had once been married to Haley appeared in the doorway.

"Pierce, I want you to meet my father, Vernon."

Chapter 11

Haley rushed through her meeting. Afterward, she called into the office to tell her boss that she had to take some time to handle personal business. With these details taken care of, she drove out of the downtown area and headed home.

Pierce had called to say that everything was fine. He hadn't elaborated. She'd invited him to come over later. After dealing with Vernon, she knew that she'd need to talk to Pierce.

She pulled into the driveway, irritated to see

Vernon's familiar convertible parked in her driveway. It gave the impression that he belonged in her home and that they were a couple. She slammed the door shut and marched into the house.

"Hi, Mom, surprise!" Beth announced.

Surprise, my foot, Haley thought. She glared at Vernon who sat on the couch with his foot elevated on a stool. The dining table was set for three. Tantalizing scents filled the air. If she wasn't mistaken, she smelled salmon, Vernon's favorite.

"Vernon, what are you doing here?"

"Mom?" Beth's voice took on a shrill tone. "I wanted Daddy to be here," she said. Beth's face begged Haley to go along with the situation. "He said that he can stay here for a couple days. I gave him the third bedroom."

"What?" Haley dropped her pocketbook to the floor. She felt a cold white fury sweep over her. "Vernon, why are you really here?"

"I missed my family," he said. He reached for Beth, who snuggled against his chest. Once, that would have been cute. Now it was a pathetic display of manipulation. Something that Vernon had perfected and she had hidden from her daughter.

"Mom, we did dinner. Like the old days."

Haley nodded, barely glancing at the table.

"Pierce stopped by earlier today," Vernon said.

She shrugged, not trusting herself to talk to Vernon about Pierce. Vernon was very perceptive and she didn't want him to guess how much she cared about Pierce.

"Seems like you're moving on with your life. I wish that I could say the same." He sighed. The sound grated on her nerves.

"Beth, could you go to your room so that I can talk with your father?"

"Sure, Mom." She leaned up and kissed her father on the cheek. "I'll go to Elaine's house and hang out for a bit. I'll be back for dinner. We can eat like a family."

Haley waited until Beth left the house before she entered the room where Vernon still sat. It irritated her that his simple gesture of leaning back in the sofa made him appear as if he belonged there. No such thing was true.

"Don't be mad at our daughter. She doesn't know how deep her mother's animosity toward her father runs," he said.

"Animosity would mean that I hate you. Vernon, I don't hate you. But my disappointment does run deep. I no longer look to you with anything close to love or like. I tolerate you for our daughter's sake. And that doesn't mean that you come into my house," she said.

She headed upstairs toward the third bedroom. His overnight bag was on the bed. She grabbed the bag and carried it down the steps. Vernon was in the kitchen, stirring various pots. She dropped the bag in the doorway of the kitchen.

"I can't stop you from staying in this town. But you won't be staying here," she said.

"Let's call a truce. Let Beth have her way for tonight." He raised his hands to stem her protest. "I will get a hotel in town for the remaining two nights. I need to make it up to her for not showing up at the hospital."

"All girlfriends busy this weekend? So you decided to squeeze Beth into your life."

The smile disappeared and a cold look came over his face. She had pushed too far, but he was on her turf now. And she wasn't quaking in her boots. She wouldn't back down.

"I'm heading out of the country in a month." He turned off the stove and removed two pots from the range. "Where are the serving dishes?"

She pointed to a cupboard above his head. So

he was going out of the country. He couldn't possibly dangle that piece of news without further explanation.

He took down a dish and stared at it. "Don't recognize these," he said.

"I replaced all my dishes."

His mouth twisted into a half grin. "Wiping me out of your life one dish at a time, huh?" He looked at the clock on the microwave. "Beth should be home soon. I told her that dinner would be at six."

"And heaven help us if we are late."

"I've mellowed," he said.

"You're going out of the country?" This softer, gentler Vernon unnerved her.

"I accepted a transfer to Spain for three years."

"Have you told Beth?"

He shook his head. "Of course, unfortunately this will affect my opportunities to visit her," he said.

She knew that some countries were more tolerant when it came to fathers obtaining custody of their children. She needed time to think.

"I was hoping to avoid all the legal claptrap. I want us to get back together. We made a good team. I think that I've changed. Looks like you have, too. We could be a unit again."

"Maybe you didn't understand me before. I don't love you," Haley said. Her heart raced and she felt a shortness of breath. Good heavens, she felt as if she were on the verge of a panic attack.

"And that's what these three days are for. We will reevaluate what we had. Then make a decision. I'm prepared to accept whatever your decision is, but I want a fighting chance."

"Mom, please, give Daddy a chance."

Haley felt as if someone had punched her in the gut. This couldn't be happening. It shouldn't be happening. Her daughter stared at her with tears shimmering in her eyes. Meanwhile, her ex-husband stood in her kitchen with a pot in his hand, scooping salmon and vegetables into a serving dish. The scene seemed pretty homey, except it wasn't her fantasy.

"Beth, give your mother a chance to recover. Let's eat," Vernon directed.

Haley sat at the table, barely eating. This was like a play that had gone awry. Vernon had taken the lead and hit on all the emotional points to manipulate the outcome. Once again, she would emerge as the bad guy when she had to break it to Beth that there would be no reunion.

"Daddy, this is delicious." Beth finished off

her plate. Something that Haley hadn't seen her do in a long time.

"I'm glad you liked it. I've been taking cooking classes," he said.

From the way he said it, Haley suspected that one of her replacements had been a chef. Well, he certainly got around.

"You don't like the meal?" Vernon asked.

"I don't have much of an appetite."

"I made your favorite dessert. Crème brûlée." Vernon went into the kitchen and retrieved little dishes of the sweet custard.

She watched him distribute the bowls around the table. This could not be happening. Vernon could not stay in this house, not for one night. She didn't trust him. If given the chance, he would try to come into her room. She didn't care how much he said that he'd changed. It was his nature to be overbearing and chauvinistic. He wouldn't understand that she didn't want him any longer.

"Beth, Vernon, thank you for going to all this trouble," Haley said with a forced smile.

"No trouble at all," Vernon replied.

"You can't stay in the house, even for one night."

"Mom, why do you have to spoil things?"

"Your father is leaving, Beth. Why don't you tell her why you came in the first place?"

Vernon explained while Beth shook her head furiously. Haley wanted to grab her and hold her, but knew that her teen daughter's emotions were volatile.

Beth shoved back her chair. "Does anyone care what I think?"

"That's why I'm here, Beth," Vernon said to Beth's retreating figure. She headed up the stairs and a minute later Haley heard Beth's door slam.

"Seems like she needs a firm hand," Vernon said.

Haley heard the criticism. If he thought that he would wear her down by battling her, then he didn't know who he was dealing with.

"Do you need directions to the nearest hotel?"

"Despite your daughter's wishes, you're going to be stubborn. Pride is a destructive vice. I hope you don't regret this later," Vernon warned her.

"I'll live with it," Beth said.

He stood over her at the dinner table. He smoothed back her hair. She cringed with each touch. Then his hand gripped the back of her neck and she gasped.

"Listen to me, Haley. I haven't forgotten that I

told you that no one is breaking us up. You want to pretend that you have the 'cojones' to deal with me. Is this new bravado because of Pierce Masterson?"

Haley pulled her head away from his hand and stood. Her chest heaved from the force of her anger. "Put a hand on me again and you'll spend the night in jail. You can't threaten me anymore. Beth is my responsibility and I'll fight you with every breath to make sure that you don't use her in your little game. Are you really going to Spain?"

"Yes."

"That's the best news I've heard in years," Haley said.

He walked over and retrieved his bag. "Maybe you think that you can re-create the family life we had with Pierce. Here's a little info that I think you should know. Pierce can never replace me in Beth's life. Trying to force him on my daughter may earn you her resentment. Can you live with that?"

"I'll be in touch," Haley said.

He opened the door a second before Pierce knocked. Both men stared at each other, long and hard. Haley remained rooted in her spot. Vernon turned and smiled at her, touching his hand to his brow in a mock salute before walking past Pierce.

Pierce stared at her. She ran into his arms and held him tight. They said nothing as they hugged in the doorway with the light from the house outlining their silhouette.

"Pierce, you're here." Beth ran up to him and hugged him. "Guess what I did yesterday."

"She painted her room orange," Haley informed Pierce.

Pierce's eyebrow shot up. "Maybe I need to move up the sale date."

Beth playfully punched him in the arm. "You'll love it. It's an orange-sherbet color and then I'm going for lime-green accents."

"Very seventies." He made a face at Haley as Beth left the room. "Did you help?" he asked softly.

She shook her head. "All Beth's idea and doing. If she had told me, I would have nixed it."

He kissed her nose. "Lucky for you that I'm sleeping with the lady of the house."

"Lucky for me that I have friends in high places. Have you heard of the great Dr. Masterson?"

"No. Tell me all about him."

"He's has a great bedside manner that makes me drool. The things that he can do with his stethoscope…" She patted his butt and winked.

"Sounds like a man after my own heart," he said.

Beth came down the stairs. "Can I go with Sandy to the movies and spend the night over at her house?"

"But we had an agreement to go to Pierce's family reunion," Haley said, reminding her daughter of their prior commitment.

"That's okay. It's just a mini-reunion with just the relatives that live in the immediate area." He could see that Beth wanted no part of being a happy threesome. He and Beth had a great relationship as long as he didn't usurp her father's position.

"Mom, I really want to go with Sandy. Her parents won't let her go to the movie alone." Beth turned up the whine.

"You're being rude, young lady," Haley said through clenched teeth.

Pierce sensed the mood was about to take a nasty turn. "Haley, it's not a problem. I'm sure Beth will be bored with all the old people reminiscing."

"See, even Pierce says it's okay. Plus it's his family."

Pierce cringed, not that he had any objections with the factual statement. It was Haley's face that made him want to take flight. Beth, however, was not flustered by her mother's furious expression. Pierce figured that Beth must be used to Haley's disapproval.

"We're leaving now. Get your butt in the car. Pierce, we're ready," Haley stated in a stern, strained voice.

Pierce rattled the car keys in his pocket and followed the mother and daughter, who argued all the way to his car.

"I wish you would stop treating me like a child. I look after myself for the better part of the day. But when you are around, you act as if I don't have any rights. Pierce, do you think that is fair?"

"I...well, I think that your mother..." Pierce looked in the rearview mirror sensing the daggers that Beth threw his way. Considering that Sheena blasted him frequently for his skills at keeping the family together, he realized he was in a lose-lose situation. Haley hadn't changed her expression to a kinder, gentler one. "I think that you should listen to your mother."

In the whole scheme of things, Haley was the one with the power.

That comment earned him an approving nod from Haley.

And from Beth, he scored a goose egg. Her eyes blazed her anger at him. He'd try talking to her later.

They arrived at the family reunion in stony silence. It looked as if the entire city had been invited to Sheena's home.

"Beth, meet us back here in two hours, at three o'clock," Haley shouted as Beth disappeared in the crowd.

"Maybe you shouldn't have forced her to come. It could be a miserable two hours," Pierce said.

"I plan to have a good time. I won't let her get away with acting like a spoiled brat," Haley replied.

"I understand, but we don't have a normal situation here."

"Are you telling me that I handled this situation incorrectly?"

"Nope. I wanted to know if you wanted a hamburger or fried chicken," he asked.

"Chicken!" She rubbed his back. "Fried chicken, please."

They headed over to the area where the food was being cooked. Over the next hour while they ate, different members of his extended family came up to be introduced to Haley. He knew that she would be the center of attention at the gathering, because he rarely brought women to meet his family.

"You've got such a big family," Haley said, her voice full of wonder.

"Don't be fooled. I don't think most of these people are my relatives."

Haley scanned the crowd. "Haven't seen Beth," she said.

"I've been keeping an eye on her. She was on the basketball court a few minutes ago."

"I hope she's going to eat," she said.

"Stay here, I'll go check on her," he said.

"Thanks."

He walked through the crowd. The basketball court and ensuing game attracted lots of teens. He was taller than most of the kids, so he could see over their heads and spotted Beth easily.

Beth was standing with a couple of kids. They moved off to the side and around a building. He followed. When he turned the corner, he saw Beth raise a cigarette to her lips.

"Put that down now," he demanded.

The cigarette jerked out of her hand as if someone had snatched it. Beth looked at him with horror.

"Don't you move," he ordered as the others ran out of his reach.

He approached Beth, not sure how hard to push. If it had been his sister, he would have dragged her to the car and driven home reading her the riot act all the way there, until her knees shook.

Haley sat in the middle of Beth's room on the floor. She pulled out each drawer, looked through her backpack and even opened her diary.

The police had already come and taken a report. Since she hadn't been kidnapped and she had voluntarily run away, the Amber alert system wasn't a consideration.

Haley had called all the friends she could identify out of Beth's address book. She wanted to cry, but knew that wouldn't help her find Beth.

"Haley!"

"Up here." Thank goodness Pierce had gotten her message.

She met him at the top of the stairs. "I drove

around, but I'm afraid to leave. She hasn't called either phone."

"Why did she leave?"

"She was mad at me for not going back with Vernon," she said.

"Guess I did not help the situation," Pierce replied.

"You're helping me." She leaned toward him. They kissed.

Suddenly Pierce pulled away. "I have a thought."

"What?"

"Come with me." Pierce ran out of the room, holding her hand. They headed to his car.

"Talk to me, Pierce. What are you thinking?"

"Don't want to get your hopes up, but I may know where she is," he said.

"Then let's go."

Haley held on to Pierce's hand. She didn't have much to say. They rode through the night. Everyone was going about their business. No one knew that her daughter was missing.

"We'll get through this."

"That's what I have to believe to keep going." She wiped away a tear and hoped that at the end of this night her daughter would be home.

They turned into his office parking lot. Haley looked around, surprised that this was where Pierce had taken her.

"Come with me." She followed him and they walked to the door.

"Why do you think she would be here?" Haley asked.

"She worked here today."

He opened the door and disabled the alarms.

Haley ran past him, calling to her daughter.

Pierce started down the hallway, opening each door. Haley ran to his office and flung open the door.

"Beth?" Her daughter had energy bars, bottled water and candy scattered around her on the floor.

Her daughter was crying. Haley ran over and scooped her into her arms. They held each other in the dark room.

An hour later, Haley was back at home. She had called the police to let them know that Beth was safe. Now it was time to get her life back on track. She put Beth to bed.

Where was the little girl who used to laugh and play without a care? This was beyond teenage hormones. Haley felt as if her family were falling apart and she didn't know what to do.

"Beth, you can always talk to me." She stroked her daughter's forehead. "I know that I've been busy, but I'll change my schedule."

"Mom, I don't need you to smother me. I know that you have to work."

"Then why did you run away? I'm trying to give you everything," she asked.

"I want us to go back to the way things were," Beth replied.

Haley didn't know how to make Beth understand that their former life was in the past. She hugged her daughter, wishing that the simple act would transfer some secret knowledge to her daughter.

"I want my father," Beth said.

Haley settled Beth into the bed. She pulled up the sheets tucking her in. "We'll talk in the morning."

Haley went to her room, feeling tired and more than a little defeated. She took a quick shower and crawled into bed. Her phone rang; she knew that it was Pierce. For the first time, she ignored the phone. Reaching over, she turned off the light and settled against the pillows.

She would have to make some serious sacrifices. She didn't know whether she had the strength to do what was necessary, but she couldn't let her daughter's world fall apart.

Pierce woke up in the morning after a restless night. He had tried to get in touch with Haley, but she hadn't answered his phone messages. She was probably dealing with Beth, which was quite understandable. He felt a little left out after they'd found Beth in his office, but he also felt guilty even thinking about his own feelings.

He jumped in his car and headed to Haley's, hoping that he could catch her before she headed to work.

He walked around to the back, expecting to see her in the kitchen. The blinds were closed. The house seemed eerily quiet. He couldn't see into the garage to know if her car was in there.

He knocked on the door.

Haley came to the door looking tired. The shadows under her eyes underscored their redness. He reached toward her and she pulled back.

"Hi, Pierce, come in."

"How is Beth?" He looked around expecting to see the young girl bursting into the room telling him about her latest adventure.

"She's still asleep. Figured that she is probably a little worn down. I called in sick to work."

"I'm heading into the office, but I'll be back as soon as I get a break. I want to be here to help you with her."

"Thanks, but it's not necessary."

"I know you're scared, but don't push me away."

"I'm not pushing you away. But it's time for me to focus on Beth. We've spent too much time together and it hasn't helped matters."

Pierce couldn't believe what he heard. Haley was pulling away from him. This couldn't be happening. He'd thought they had turned a corner.

"Pierce, I'm going to have to ask that we separate for a little while," she said and looked at him for understanding.

He had none. His defenses went up, sensing that he could not hold her trust.

"You're right, of course. You need to focus on your family and I need to do the same with mine."

Chapter 12

Pierce stood at the bottom of the driveway collecting the day's mail. The summer evenings had vanished and a decided nip was in the early-afternoon air. Hampton Mews could have harsh winters and forecasters predicted a bad winter season. Extreme weather resulted in specific ailments for his patients. Summer brought in victims of heat stroke and dehydration. Winter saw heart attacks from shoveling snow and mild cases of frostbite on fingers and toes.

A survey of his cul-de-sac showed that his

neighbors had set their trash bins at the curb for the next day's trash pickup. He supposed that he'd better bring out the trash from his house this evening. In the morning, he would bring it to the curb. Raccoons loved his trash, knocking the bins over and rummaging through their contents. The animals didn't seem to bother anyone else's trash.

He looked at his watch. It was getting close to dinnertime.

Since it was only him, he didn't have a schedule planned around meals. The reality stung, but he'd get over the disappointment. At least, his choice for dinner didn't have to be vetted by a wife and daughter. He didn't have to cook dinner for his wife who might flex her muscles and declare *his* kitchen as *her* turf. He wouldn't have to hear his child whine about the dinner selection. He had what he needed: one bowl, a spoon, one can of chicken soup and a microwave.

"Whoo hoo, Dr. Masterson." Mrs. Saltzberg, his next-door neighbor, waved in greeting.

Pierce tapped the mail to his forehead in a farewell salute. Standing outside with Mrs. Saltzberg until the sun set and sank below the horizon didn't appeal to him. He confessed to feeling grumpier than usual lately.

Mrs. Saltzberg would have him discussing the toilet habits of the neighbor's German shepherd, the mayor's decision to scale back recycling pickup from two days to one and the state of "undress" of the neighborhood teens.

Most days he could indulge her with conversation, but not tonight. His head began to throb when he saw her come farther down her driveway and head up the sidewalk toward him. Through his headache haze, he saw her enhanced red hair in its usual frizzy mop, her floral housecoat and white walking shoes coming at him.

"Haven't seen you in a bit. Everything okay?"

"No problems, here." He backed up onto his driveway, with the feeling that having his property under his feet gave him hope that he'd be heading into his house in a few minutes. On a couple of occasions, she'd followed him into his house and then had called her husband over to see the place. With neighbors like her, he couldn't feel lonely if he tried.

"I always keep an eye on the house when you're gone. You've been gone a lot, way past your office hours," Mrs. Saltzberg probed.

"Thank you. You're very thoughtful. What would I do without you?" He brushed away an annoying gnat that buzzed around his face. His headache hadn't let up.

"I thought, maybe, that you'd found a young lady." She twittered, but her curious gaze fastened onto his face. "I saw Jean in the grocery store and we chatted."

Pierce switched his attention from the gnat to Mrs. Saltzberg. His employee gossiped about him while shopping in a grocery store? He realized that the indiscretion was normal employee behavior, but having his workers gossip about him was not acceptable. Unfortunately, this was a small city. And what went around, came around. The flaming redhead in front of him pestering him about his private life served to prove his case.

Where was an ice-cream truck when you needed one?

Instead he faced his neighbor's questions. Mrs. Saltzberg didn't have a reputation for diplomacy. Her direct questions didn't suffer misinterpretations.

"Come to think of it, Mr. Masterson, I've never seen you bring a young lady home. And what a beautiful home you have. Or is it that you're afraid she'll want the house more than she'll want you." She chortled. Her face bunched from appreciation of her humor.

He shook his head. "Sorry to disappointment you, Mrs. Saltzberg. There's no woman out there for me. I'm actually waiting for you to fall for me." He'd embarrassed her into silence. He didn't crack a smile. Good.

"I'll be talking to you later," he said, and quickly walked up his driveway. She'd stepped on his toes with her probing questions. Now wasn't the time to deal with any topic that reminded him that his relationship with Haley was over, completely dead.

He slammed his front door shut and the sound echoed through the large house. For some reason, the sound irritated him. A big, empty house to accompany his big, empty heart. He fanned the mail in his hand, examining the return addresses to determine their importance. Nothing but bills and junk mail. He tossed the letters onto the side table, where they sat with the piles from previous days. Maybe he'd get Laura to help him sort through and pay the bills that needed immediate attention.

Laura was mad at him, because she blamed him for his breakup with Haley. He'd have to wait a week or so to approach her. What had his life come to, he wondered, when even his strongest ally had turned her back on him.

The last few nights had been torture. During the day, he was busy with patients and office issues to keep his thoughts from drifting. The wall mural didn't help his concentration. It was a constant reminder of the Sanders family. He'd started using the back door to minimize thinking about Beth, or wondering about her latest exploits.

He opened his cabinet and searched through the cans in the cupboard and found some chicken soup. Beth's favorite term—*loser*—applied to him. In a matter of months, his life was defined by when he met Haley and when he'd broken up with her. Prior to Haley, he'd eaten salads because whenever he cooked, the volume resulted in leftovers for an entire week.

If he'd cooked his family's favorite meals, he'd call them over for dinner. They'd get a good meal and he would have company. This arrangement had worked until he'd mentioned selling the house and advised Omar to go back to school.

The microwave hummed to life after he placed the bowl of soup in it. Now he was reduced to eating canned soup because fixing dinner wouldn't be the same without sharing it with family…or with Haley and Beth.

He took out the steaming soup carefully and headed for the couch. Maybe he'd read the newspaper or bore himself to sleep by watching TV tonight. Neither option appealed to him. He placed a cushion on his lap and sipped his soup. Tomorrow he'd check with Morton to see if he wanted to go to lunch or dinner, or both. Maybe he could convince Morton to come over for a game of chess.

Morton would get on his case about Haley. She'd wrapped his friend around her finger just as she'd wrapped herself around his heart. Morton had gushed about how intelligent she was and a what good conversationalist she was.

Pierce thought about how he would break the news to Morton about Haley. He'd start off with the fact that it was a mutual separation. Breaking up with Haley was for the best. It was practical. Haley and he were acting like adults. She needed to concentrate on her family and he needed to do the same with his.

The phone rang. He wasn't moving. His salty soup was half-eaten. He moved it to the side table. Although he wasn't going to answer the phone, he still was curious about the caller. He didn't expect Haley to call, unless she'd forgotten an important cooking tip or needed his medical expertise.

The ringing stopped before the answering machine clicked on. He stared at the black box, then noticed the blinking light. The display showed three messages. He pressed the play button. A weak flicker of hope flashed expectantly, and then burned out in a hollow poof when he identified the caller.

"Pierce, are you there? Call me. You're such an idiot." He hit the erase button. He wasn't in the mood for fighting with Sheena. He could guess what she was fired up about, but he wasn't in the mood.

"Pierce, I know you're there. Where else would a moron be?"

What was wrong with Sheena? He erased that message and went on to the next one, which he sensed was also from Sheena. So much for thinking that Haley would call him. "I can't believe that you're my brother. Guess you got one hundred percent of the stupid gene. I'm coming over and don't bother pretending that you're not at home." His finger poised ready to erase

Sheena's tirade. First, however, he would determine what time the message had come through so he could figure out how much time he had to escape.

The message came in at 6:00 p.m. The clock on the microwave showed 6:27 p.m. Crap. Sheena only lived fifteen minutes away with traffic.

No one had to witness his retreat. He refused to use the word *cowardly*. All he was doing was setting the boundaries of his personal space. Since the warrior queen had announced her attack, he had to move his personal space to higher ground. Grabbing his keys and his wallet, he headed for the garage, listening for any signs that she'd pulled up to the house.

He started the car and punched in the button to open the garage. "All these darn women are going to give me a heart attack." He shifted the car into Reverse, waiting for the right amount of space between his car and the garage door before he floored the gas.

A familiar dark blue minivan roared up the street before, tires squealing, it blocked his car. He slammed on his brakes.

"Sheena, move your car!" he shouted, staring at hers through the rearview mirror.

Instead of obeying, Sheena stepped out of the car. She blocked his escape and he had no alternate plan to deal with her. Pierce leaned his head back and closed his eyes in frustration and defeat.

Where was Mrs. Saltzberg when he needed her? he wondered. He knew the answer. She probably sat staring out the window taking in every detail and eating popcorn while she enjoyed the show.

A sharp knock on his window startled him. Sheena and Carlton Jr. looked in at him. Sheena glared and Junior stared. He could pretend not to understand her and motion that he couldn't hear her. He knew that the scene, despite its humorous points, would raise her temper to the point where she'd start shouting at him through the window of the car as he sat in the driveway. And he'd earn a citation from his strict home owners' association.

He waved her away from the car so he could emerge.

"I just came from Haley's. I needed to talk to you and figured you would be over there," Sheena said.

"I don't live there." *Anymore.*

"Before yesterday, I would've called you a liar

because you were always there, even when she wasn't home," Sheena said.

His nephew sipped from a juice box. When he squeezed the box, juice squirted from the bent straw onto Sheena's shoe. She didn't notice. Junior looked worried that his mother would make the discovery. *I've got your back, little man.* Pierce patted his head and winked at the young boy. *And that's what uncles with mean sisters were for,* he wanted to explain to his nephew.

"Sheena, I'm tired and I have lots to do. What do you want?"

"What? Tired of being a jerk? And I don't really care where you were running off to. I'm not going to let you mess up your life. See, I'm going to play your role in this little drama that you've created," she explained.

"As usual, you don't know what you are talking about. But that has never stopped you from jumping right in," he told her. He resumed playing with his nephew, tickling him under his chin. Carlton Jr. giggled and ran around their legs. Playing tag was so much more fun than being chewed out.

"Come on, Carlton. I've got your favorite cookies all ready for you," Pierce said to the boy.

He refused to continue this conversation on his sidewalk. He took his nephew's hand and led him into the house. Unfortunately, he heard Sheena's footsteps and, if he concentrated, he'd feel her breath on the back of his neck. She was like a fire-breathing dragon. She was muttering something about the size of his head.

Pierce had a routine when his nephew visited. He retrieved the box of his favorite cookies and placed a few on a plate with a large glass of milk. His nephew thanked him in his cartoon-character voice and settled in to enjoy his favorite chair, a kid-size reclining chair, in the family room.

"Didn't know you had one of those." Sheena walked closer to inspect the burgundy-colored, upholstered chair.

"I'm prepared to give my nephew whatever he needs when he visits, which isn't often enough." He'd loved Carlton Jr. from the first day Sheena had declared that she was pregnant. As Carlton got older, Pierce couldn't help thinking about the day when he would have his son or daughter. "When are you going to have another child?"

Sheena looked thrown off by the question and then she smiled. He wondered if there would soon be an addition to his sister's family. She was a great mother. He wondered if he would be as good a father. Thoughts of parenting shifted his thoughts to their father.

He had come to the realization that his father had played a crucial role in his family's development. Pierce had been sixteen years old when his father had left, but remembered camping in the backyard looking up at the stars with his dad. He and his father had taken a trip to the mountains where they'd gone white water rafting. That trip had been their last. It had been exactly a month before he'd disappeared from his life.

On that last day, his father had driven toward the house where Pierce had waited to play catch with Omar. The girls had gone to visit their friends. His mother had been in the kitchen fixing dinner. The Crown Victoria had cruised past Pierce, never stopping, but had slowed enough for him to see his father do a single wave. Pierce had remained at that spot until the car had disappeared from the intersection.

When Omar had come out, Pierce had played with him, not like a big brother with his annoying kid brother. He'd played with him as he thought a father would play with his son. From that day, he'd wanted to shield his family from the pain of betrayal and the guilt of his foreknowledge of their father's desertion.

"I wish that Haley could see you like this."

"Like what?" Pierce tore himself from his maudlin thoughts. Any mention of Haley tended to grabbed his attention.

"Sensitive. Human. Not trying to be the man who knows everything or has done everything," she said. He pulled her by her arm before she finished her sentence. Carlton didn't need to see him argue with his mother. They stood face-to-face in the living room.

"I didn't get any complaints from Haley. Since I'm not going out with you, then your opinion doesn't really count. What does Haley have to do with you?"

"Why did you break up with her? Did she cheat on you?" Sheena took a seat, crossed her legs and folded her arms.

"Where do you get your information?"

"Okay, let's try another question. Did you cheat on her?"

"Sheena, I'm tired." He flung up his hands in surrender. "I don't want to play your games tonight. Neither Haley nor I cheated on the other."

His sister was wearing out her already thin welcome.

"See, I think that you did cheat on her. You're the type of man to do that," Sheena said.

"On second thoughts, maybe you shouldn't have another child. I think your brain is leaking good sense." Her accusation insulted him. "Sheena, this was a mutual decision between Haley and me. We are two adults who knew better than to pretend we were in some fantasy land, instead of being responsible."

"Here's a news flash. You're not a parent. You never were a parent. And at the rate that you're going, you may never be a parent." Sheena's leg started its swinging, a sure sign that she was only getting started. "You cheated on Haley with us. We are your convenient tool. Between work and your family, you don't have to deal with your life. You don't have to gamble on having a relationship. You don't have to screw up and fail. You don't have to get your heart broken. You don't have to be a quitter and walk out like Dad," she said. "Pierce, don't be scared to love."

"I can't take much more of this. My head hurts. I'm happy to see my nephew, but I'm going to have to ask you to leave." Pierce needed air. Everything crowded in on him. The walls with their decorations, the bulky furniture, the large TV. His sister pointing at him didn't help. All he wanted to know was when she would stop.

"I don't know why you made yourself into the martyr. Mom had moved on. Sure she hurt and cried, but she didn't waste her life pining away after Dad left. Have you conveniently forgotten that she had male friends? She may have always compared them to Dad because she never remarried, but the point is that she didn't give into her fears, at least not completely, or stop living and loving."

His sister came forward and touched him on his shoulder. He couldn't remember the last time that they had touched, much less hugged. "You've helped us, but you've also used us to build a fortress around your heart. It's time to let us go. Omar will make you proud, whatever he decides to do. I do have my doubts about his success, but he's got to live his life. Laura lives and breathes for her big brother's approval. One day she'll find that special someone. And you know me. I take things one day at a time.

"It's time for you to release us and free yourself from the burden of thinking that you have to carry us on your back for all eternity," she said quietly.

Anger mixed with sadness, shock and then with happiness. His emotions swirled out of control. He didn't like feeling as if he had no options. "I've made my decision. I can live with it. I suggest that you try to do the same. Focus on you and yours," Pierce said. He stepped back.

Replacing the distance between them helped him regain his balance. "Refresh my memory, but I do recall you not liking Haley when you found out that she would buy the house. You had unjustly accused her of wanting a meal ticket and a father for her child. Then you embarrassed her at your barbecue. Don't pretend that all of a sudden you give a damn about her and her feelings," he accused.

"I've made my apologies. She may not see me as a friend as yet, but she sees me as someone who speaks candidly. I told her that you loved her and that your love scared you," she said.

"Have you lost your mind? How dare you?" he blustered, looking for the right words to blast her out of his house.

"Do you love her?" Sheena demanded.

He nodded.

"I didn't hear you," she prodded.

"Yes," he said.

"Then what else matters?"

"I may not be able to make her happy." The simple confession depleted him. He took a seat on the bottom step of the central staircase. He rested his aching forehead on his crossed arms.

"And why do you think that's your sole responsibility?"

Pierce's head snapped up. Haley stood in front of him. He stared at her openmouthed, vaguely wondering if his sister's assault had sent him into a state of hallucination.

"I think this is my cue to leave," Sheena said and called to her son. "No need to call me for a pickup. I already know how this will work out." She walked over and planted a kiss on his cheek. "See, big brother, you aren't the only one with mother hen instincts." She leaned close to his ear. "Don't screw this up. I like her." With that comment, Sheena nodded toward Haley and exited with her son in tow.

"How long have you been standing there?" He didn't have the strength to move from his seat. His bone-weary exhaustion had been replaced by deep surprise and a rising excitement that teetered on ecstatic delirium.

"Lucky me. Sheena came to my house first, lectured me, then demanded that I get in her van. I really thought that I was being kidnapped. Didn't know we were coming here. Can't say that I would've come even if she'd threatened me." Haley eyed him, as if waiting for his response. His mind hadn't gotten over the surprise of her appearance. She continued, "When I saw you in the driveway, I knew that every word your sister spoke, might I add at the top of her lungs, was true. I was afraid that, if you saw me, you wouldn't listen to her, or me. But once you saw Carlton Jr., you didn't focus on anything else," she said.

His demeanor softened at the thought of being seen playing with his nephew. Spending time with Carlton was one of the few times that he didn't have to assume a role. At times he yearned for his nephew's innocence.

"Do you want me to stay?"

"Yes," he said quietly.

She sat next to him, slipping her hand around his arm. Her hair fell across his shoulder. He leaned closer, drawing in her scent. There were so many things that he remembered about this woman. The minute he heard her voice, his resolve disintegrated like fine powder. How could she do this? They'd agreed to go their separate ways. He hung his head in shame. The accusations he'd flung at her haunted him.

"Oh, Pierce, talk to me. What went wrong?" Haley draped an arm over his shoulder, resting her cheek against his body. "I heard most of what Sheena said, but I know that this isn't a one-way street. I had my fears, too."

"No," he said softly. "Sheena was right, but don't tell her I said so," he said and grimaced. Suddenly, he pulled Haley against his chest. He had used his father's actions to set up a ghost in the closet of his emotions. And to think that he had given it so much power that he almost walked away from the only woman who had scaled that ten-foot wall around his heart and conquered him.

"You know what I was afraid of?" Haley looked up in his face. He shook his head. "After having such a messy marriage, I wanted to make things as perfect as possible the next time around. I wanted to pave the rest of Beth's life with no problems, no issues and no disappointments. But life doesn't quite work that way. Our relationship didn't go along a set course. I was in some kind of fantasy while my daughter got sick. And I took my fear out on you." Haley's eyes glistened with tears. She wiped away a few that had spilled down her cheek.

He kissed each eyelid, wishing that he could stop the cause of her pain. But he had to learn to give her the space to express her emotions.

"I felt guilty about feeling so happy in your company. Boy, and when you sat across from me over a romantic dinner, I thought it wasn't right or fair, because my daughter was hurting. I'd promised her this rosy garden, but couldn't keep up my end of the deal."

"That's why we'll do this together. No more superheroes," he assured her. "Haley, you are my rock."

"And you're my reality and my future," she said.

Night had fallen. Dinnertime had passed. The outside world and its goings-on didn't matter. His life, his love, sat next to him. He opened his hand and she laid hers in his. Together they could help each other heal.

He kissed her, stopping short of the emotional avalanche that could quickly overcome him. "Let's raid the kitchen. I may have ice cream and some whip cream."

"I never asked, but who decorated your house?" Haley patted the bar stool at the counter of the kitchen.

"My sisters. You don't like it?"

"It's efficient, but not really you. Isn't your favorite color blue? Yet there is no shade of blue anywhere in this house."

"Sheena doesn't like blue." He shrugged, making a face. "Madame Critic, are you up to the challenge?"

Haley fed him a spoon of the vanilla ice cream. He rolled his eyes in contentment. Kissing her lips after each spoonful of ice cream, he enjoyed the hot and cool sensations. If she'd let him, he'd alternate a kiss with each mouthful of treat until the freezer was empty of ice cream.

"Can't believe that Sheena offered to babysit Beth."

"She's trying to make up for your rocky start."

"It's okay. I know that she was being protective. I'd be that way with my brothers, although they seem to be able to handle themselves where the women are concerned. I'm the one who seems to need help in the romance department."

"Hope you haven't had to call them about me."

She snuggled against his chest. He loved the

smell of her hair. He ran his fingers through it, massaging her neck.

"I did call them."

"And…"

"I think that's between me and my brothers."

"Then I'm going to have to interrogate you and get you to tell the truth."

"All yours, big boy." She unwrapped his arms from around her and slid to the other side of the couch.

"Did I tell you that I'm uniquely qualified for this task of debriefing you?"

"So you keep saying. I think that you've met your match." She stood and moved around to the back of the couch. Pierce didn't move, aware that their game of seduction had begun. He resisted the urge to pull her down into his arms. She was playing dirty and he liked it.

"Why don't you meet me upstairs?"

She trailed her finger along his shoulder, over his back to the next shoulder. She pressed her breast against his arm and blew in his ear.

If he was a puppy, he'd be running in circles. His tail would wag furiously as he waited to jump on top of Haley. As man's best friend, he'd get to lick her for a vigorous ear rub.

His fingers gripped the edge of the couch. How had she turned the tables? Maybe he had never been in charge. From her seductive tone, he'd say that she'd been in control all along.

Haley called down to him. He hurried to the stairs.

"You bad, bad woman." He turned to see her naked back go around the corner. Her blouse was lying on the floor discarded.

Now that he knew her destination, he didn't hurry to follow. It made the moment all the more exciting. He picked up her shirt, enjoying the feel of the silky fabric between his fingers.

In the hallway on a bust, she had left her bra. He picked it up with a finger and tossed it on top of the shirt in his other hand.

"Pierce, you dear *old* man, what's taking you so long? Are the stairs too much for you?" Her laughter floated in the air. The raised ceiling added a sultry echo to her ringing laugh.

He passed her shoes on the way, then blue slacks. By the time he reached the room, he was panting.

All the doors along the hall had been closed, except for one. The door to his bedroom stood open. It was the only door that faced him. Since it was the width of the house, there was enough room for her to play hide-and-seek in the suite. He hoped that she'd have mercy on him. He didn't want to rip the room apart looking for her.

Soft music wafted from the room. As he got closer, he recognized the alluring tones of Nina Simone.

He pushed open the door. To his left in the small sitting room there was no sign of Haley. In the middle of the room, his chest of drawers and bureau lined the walls. On the right was his king-size sleigh bed. Sheena had insisted on the cranberry-red décor, not allowing him his first choice of forest-green and maroon. Despite his objections, she had zoomed in and installed the color and all the decorations in one day.

He opened the two walk-in closets, expecting Haley to jump out at him. Then he heard the faint sound of a shower. He smiled.

His bathroom was the size of a standard bedroom. He approached the shower stall. The cloud of steam hovered over the opening before being eliminated by the fan.

The door swung open. She emerged naked, wet and too damned sexy.

"Love the shower cap," he teased.

"It's a new fashion trend." She pulled the plastic bag off her head that protected her hair. "Are you just going to stand there, or are you going to come to dry me." She tossed the towel to him.

Pierce threw the towel aside, tossed her over his shoulder and went to the bed where he laid her against the thick comforter. "Why waste the energy?" He covered her body with his and covered her lips with his.

He ran his hands down her sides, locking into memory every curve and nuance from the roundness of her breasts to her narrow waist to her sensuous curve of hips. Once he had covered the exterior, he wanted to explore below the surface. His hand ran down the outside of her thigh and up toward the inside. He felt her tremble as he followed the line of her muscle until he brushed against the sensitive folds that spoke to him with a moist greeting.

Haley arched against him, moaning, clawing her way up the sheets. He sucked his way from her neck down to her breast. The brown nipple brushed against his cheek. Haley ran her fingers through his hair, begging him to take her. He blew gently against her nipple, feeding it with his warm breath and then letting the coolness of the room have its effect. He played this game, while his fingers thrilled her.

She rubbed against his fingers. He obliged her because he needed to enjoy the feel of her. He slid inside, playing with her with the expertise of a concert pianist.

"Don't make me...come," she said and moaned.

"On one condition." For heaven's sake, he heard the squeak of his voice. He couldn't play the game of interrogator too much longer or he'd be begging her.

"What do you want to know?"

"Aah, there's still some fight left in you," he said and covered her nipple, teasing the hard peak with his tongue, letting his teeth graze the peak before swirling his tongue around it.

"I told my brothers that I love you," she shouted.

He didn't have to ask her to repeat the words. She'd said them in a passionate confession with the purity of truth.

With her help, he pushed down his pants, unleashing his arousal. She wrapped her hand around him, stroking him with a wicked smile.

"Now I want to know why your sister is being so nice to me," she said.

"Be-because… Damn it, Haley, don't do that." He grabbed her hand. The woman was trying to kill him. His breathing grew ragged. His heartbeat pounded in his head. All his muscles had tightened as if readying for an explosion.

He stared deep into her hazel eyes, drowning, falling, seeking their warm depths. She scooted under him and then guided him until she wrapped her legs around his hips.

"Do I still need to confess?"

"No, darling. I won't force you to say what you can't say without me rubbing myself against you." She continued the rubbing. She quivered against him, welcoming him to enter.

He grabbed onto the one thing that could make him do the right thing. He thought about his father, the man who had walked away from the family. He pushed himself away from Haley, away from her touch and applied the condom. He sat on his knees looking down at her perplexed face.

"Listen to me, Haley." His chest heaved with the effort of resisting her, but also at facing his fear. "I want you right now, so badly that I can't think. But I want you to know that I love you. When you came at me with the rake on that first day, you intrigued me. I admired your strength. I know you think that you were weak to stay with your husband as long as you did. But you're wrong. You had priorities, you had a plan. It took courage to remain focused and make sacrifices until the time was right. I never wanted to make us anything more than casual friends. I didn't want to disappoint you. But most of all I didn't want to make promises that I couldn't fulfill," he said in a strained whisper.

"Don't sell yourself short, Pierce. I've watched you with your family. I've seen you handle your patients. I've seen you with Beth. You have the kind heart of a decent man with high principles and lots of love. There is no doubt that you are man enough for me," she assured him.

"And that's why I can say what I've been afraid to say," he said. "I love you. I want you to be at my side for all time. I want to be a part of your life with Beth." He took a deep breath.

"I told Sheena that for the first time, I was willing to let go of our father's ghost and move on with my life. The fear of failure, the guarantee of true love…I blamed him for leaving that legacy with me. But, Haley, I love you."

Pierce lowered himself onto her, into her. They hugged each other in a tight embrace. Their tears mixed with their cries of rapture.

And that was the end of any logical thought.

FORGED OF STEELE

The sizzling miniseries from
USA TODAY bestselling author

BRENDA JACKSON

*Sebastian Steele's takeover of
Jocelyn Mason's fledgling company
topples when Jocelyn takes over
Sebastian's heart*

NIGHT HEAT

AVAILABLE SEPTEMBER 2006
FROM KIMANI™ ROMANCE

Love's Ultimate Destination

AVAILABLE JANUARY 2007
BEYOND TEMPTATION

Available at your favorite retail outlet.

Leila Owens didn't know
how to love herself let alone
an abandoned baby
but Garret Grayson knew
how to love them both.

She's My Baby

Adrianne Byrd

(Kimani Romance #10)

AVAILABLE SEPTEMBER 2006

FROM KIMANI™ ROMANCE

Love's Ultimate Destination

Available at your favorite retail outlet.

He found *trouble* in paradise.

Mason Sinclair's visit to Barbados
was supposed to be about uncovering
family mysteries not the mysteries of
Lianne Thomas's heart.

EMBRACING
THE MOONLIGHT
(Kimani Romance #12)

Wayne Jordan

AVAILABLE SEPTEMBER 2006
FROM KIMANI™ ROMANCE
Love's Ultimate Destination

Silhouette®

Desire®

Introducing an exciting appearance
by legendary
New York Times bestselling author

DIANA PALMER

HEARTBREAKER

He's the ultimate bachelor...
but he may have just met
the one woman to change his ways!

Join the drama in the story of a confirmed
bachelor, an amnesiac beauty and their
unexpected passionate romance.

"Diana Palmer is a mesmerizing storyteller
who captures the essence of what
a romance should be."—*Affaire de Coeur*

---

*Heartbreaker is available from Silhouette Desire
in September 2006.*

Introducing…

nocturne

a spine-tingling new line from Silhouette Books.

These paranormal romances will
seduce you with dark, passionate tales
that stretch the boundaries of conflict,
desire, and life and death, weaving
a tapestry of sensual thrills and chills!

Don't miss the first book…

UNFORGIVEN

by *USA TODAY* bestselling author

LINDSAY McKENNA

*Launching October 2006,
wherever books are sold.*